When the hairs on his nape stood up, he knew that Kathleen had come into the kitchen.

Gideon felt her gaze and straightened his shoulders, resisting the urge to peer back at her. He dated women all the time, but none of them had caught his attention the way she had.

Deep down he sensed a connection, as if she knew what it was to be hurt deeply and had held herself back from others because of that. Like him. Was that why he got the bright idea to bring dinner to her tonight?

No, it was her sons. They reminded Gideon of himself and his younger brother growing up.

He pivoted toward her, transfixed by the soft blue of her eyes. *Run.* The word set off an alarm bell in his mind. His chest constricted.

In the distance he heard her son Kip speaking to him, but Gideon couldn't tear his eyes from Kathleen, her delicate features forming a beautiful picture that could haunt him if he allowed her to get too close. But he wouldn't do that.

Books by Margaret Daley

MARGARET DALEY

feels she has been blessed. She has been married more than thirty years to her husband, Mike, whom she met in college. He is a terrific support and her best friend. They have one son, Shaun. Margaret has been writing for many years and loves to tell a story. When she was a little girl, she would play with her dolls and make up stories about their lives. Now she writes these stories down. She especially enjoys weaving stories about families and how faith in God can sustain a person when things get tough. When she isn't writing, she is fortunate to be a teacher for students with special needs. Margaret has taught for more than twenty years and loves working with her students. She has also been a Special Olympics coach and has participated in many sports with her students.

His Holiday Family
Margaret Daley

Love Inspired

™ LOVE INSPIRED BOOKS

ISBN-13: 978-0-373-81590-6

HIS HOLIDAY FAMILY

www.LoveInspiredBooks.com

Printed in U.S.A.

Therefore my heart is glad, and my glory rejoiceth: my flesh also shall rest in hope.
—*Psalms* 16:9

To Joe, thank you for your support

Chapter One

Gideon O'Brien hopped down from Engine Two and assessed the chaos in front of him. Strapping on his air pack, he started toward his captain. A hand gripped his arm and stopped his forward progress. He turned toward the blonde woman who held him, her large blue eyes glistening with tears. She looked familiar, but he couldn't place where he knew her from. His neighbor's daughter, perhaps?

"My two sons and my cousin—their babysitter—must still be inside. I don't see them outside with the other tenants." Her voice quivered. She tightened her hand on his arm and scanned the crowd. "I'm Kathleen Hart. My sons are Jared and Kip. I tried Sally's cell but she didn't answer. Please get them out." A tear slipped down her cheek.

"Where are they?" Gideon moved toward his

captain, his palm at the small of her back, guiding her in the direction he wanted her to go. Yes, he realized, she was his neighbor Ruth Coleman's daughter.

"Sally's second-floor apartment is on the east side, the fourth one down on your right. Number 212. Hurry." Her round eyes fastened on the fire consuming the three-story apartment building on Magnolia Street.

Gideon paused in front of Captain Fox. "Mrs. Hart says her sons and babysitter are still inside. Pete and I can go in and get them." He looked toward the west end of the large structure where the men of Engine One were fighting the flames eating their way through the top level. "There's still time."

"Okay." His captain surveyed the east end. "But hurry. It won't be long before this whole building goes up."

The scent of smoke hung heavy in the air. The hissing sound of water hitting Magnolia Street Apartments vied with the roar of the blaze. Gideon turned toward the mother of the two boys. "We'll find them." He gave her a smile then searched the firefighters for Pete.

When Gideon found him a few feet away, he covered the distance quickly. "Let's go. There are three people trapped on the second floor. East end."

At the main entrance into the building Gideon fixed his mask in place, glancing back at the blonde woman standing near his captain. He had seen that same look of fear and worry many times over his career as a firefighter. He wouldn't let anything happen to her sons and Sally.

Gideon switched on his voice amplifier and headed into the furnace with Pete following close behind him. Through the thick cloud suspended from the ceiling in the foyer, the stairs to the second floor loomed. Crouching, he scrambled up the steps. The higher he went, the hotter it became.

On the landing, he peered to the right, a wall of steely smoke obscuring his view. To the left, the way he needed to go, the gunmetal gray fog hovered in the hallway, denser at the top.

Gideon dropped to his hands and knees and crawled toward Sally's apartment. Sweat coated his body from the adrenaline pumping through him and the soaring temperature. The building groaned. Visibility only three feet in front of him, he hugged the wall, his heart pounding. He sucked air into his lungs, conscious of the limited amount of oxygen in his tank.

Calm down. Not much time. In and out.

Mindful of every inhalation, he counted the doors they passed in the corridor. One. Two.

Three. The next apartment was Sally's. His breathing evened out as he neared his goal.

At number 212's door, Gideon tried the handle. Locked. He rose and swung his ax into the wooden obstruction, the sound of it striking its target reverberating in the smoke-filled air.

When a big enough hole appeared, Pete reached inside and opened the door. A pearly haze, not as heavy as in the corridor, engulfed the room. His partner rushed into the apartment, Gideon right behind him. In the small foyer, he noticed a large television on in the living room but didn't see anyone in there.

"I'll take the left. You the right," Gideon said, making his way down the short hallway to the first bedroom. "Fire department, is anyone here?" His gaze riveted to a double bed. He quickly searched everywhere two young boys might hide. Nothing.

For a few seconds a memory intruded into his mind, taking his focus off what needed to be done. He shoved it away, went back in the hall and crossed to the other bedroom. After checking it, he came back out into the corridor and opened the last door to a bathroom. Empty.

He pictured his neighbor's daughter next to his captain, waiting for them to bring her sons out safely. The thought that he might not be able to quickened his breathing for a moment.

When he met up with Pete in the small entryway, his partner said, "All clear in the kitchen as well as the living and dining rooms."

"The same in the bedrooms."

"Gideon, Pete, get out. Mrs. Hart sees her children and their babysitter. They just arrived and are safe," his captain's deep gravelly voice came over the radio.

"We're on our way." Relieved the two boys and Sally were all right, Gideon and Pete made their way back into the main hallway.

The smoke had grown thicker, darker. The crackling and popping sounds of the fire overrode the rumbling noise from the water continually bombarding the structure. A warning went off, signaling Pete only had five minutes of air left in his tank.

Our time is running out.

As those words flashed into Gideon's thoughts, his breathing sped up for a few seconds before he reined it in. He'd been in similar situations. They would make it.

Gideon gestured to his friend to go first. Every second counted. Pete came out of the apartment and got down on all fours, hurriedly heading for the stairs. Gideon crept along a body length behind his partner. As he crawled past the second apartment, his low-pressure air alarm alerted him to the need to move even faster.

But the nearer he came to the stairs, the soupier his surroundings were. He barely made out the back of Pete only a foot in front of him.

Gideon's shoulder brushed against the door frame of the apartment nearest to the steps. Almost there. His inhalations slowed even more to conserve as much oxygen as possible. But heat warmed the inside of his protective suit, and sweat rolled down his face. Its salty drops stung his eyes. He blinked, his vision blurring for a few seconds.

Then suddenly from above, wood and debris came tumbling down. Gideon lost sight of Pete in the dense smoke and dust. The crashing sound of a beam boomed through the air.

Lord, help.

Rolling onto his back, Gideon reached for his radio when another metallic moan cut through the noise of the fire. A piece of timber landed across his chest, knocking his radio from his hand. A sharp pain lanced a path through his upper torso. Then a second slab of lumber fell on top of the first. Gideon stared up as the rest of the ceiling plummeted. Air rushed out of his lungs, and blackness swirled before his eyes.

Holding her two sons' hands, Kathleen Hart watched them carry a firefighter out of the burning building. Fear bombarded her from all sides.

He could die because she'd mistakenly thought her children and Sally were inside. She relived the few seconds when she'd seen Jared and Kip racing toward her with Sally Nance right behind them. The elation they weren't trapped took hold. Then the knowledge she had unnecessarily sent two men into a blaze to find the trio swept away the joy. Now one of them was injured. Because of her.

She turned to Sally. "Please keep the boys with you. I need to see how the firefighter is doing."

"Sure. I'm so sorry you didn't realize I took Jared and Kip to the park. When the weather's good, we've been doing that. With the storm coming, I didn't know when we would get another chance anytime soon. I never in a thousand years thought my apartment building would catch fire and…" Her cousin gulped back the rest of her words and stared at the man on the stretcher being attended to by the paramedics.

"I know, Sally." Kathleen looked down at her sons, whose eyes were round and huge in their pale faces. "We'll talk later." She squeezed their hands gently, drawing their attention. "Stay with Sally. I'm going to check on the firefighter."

Tears shone in Kip's eyes. "Tell him we're sorry."

She stooped and grasped her nine-year-old's upper arms. "Honey, it isn't your fault."

And it isn't my fault, either. It was an unfortunate accident. If only she could believe that.

Even knowing that in her mind didn't make her feel any better as she rose and headed toward the ambulance into which the paramedics were loading the firefighter.

One of the paramedics hopped into the back of the emergency vehicle while the other shut the doors and started toward the front of the truck. She knew the paramedic because she worked as a nurse at Hope Memorial Hospital. Kathleen hurried her steps and caught up with the driver before he climbed into the cab.

"How is he, Samuel?"

"O'Brien may have some internal injuries." Samuel gave her a once-over. "Did you just come from the hospital?"

Still dressed in her scrubs, Kathleen nodded. "Will he make it?"

"He should, barring any complications." The paramedic jumped up into the ambulance.

Kathleen backed away from the vehicle and watched it leave the scene. She squeezed her eyes closed, still seeing the flashing lights in her mind. She couldn't shake the tragedy of the situation— one she'd had a part in. Just like another one, not long ago.

She tried to clear her mind of the memory. When would this go away?

Someone tugged on her arm. She looked down at Jared, her seven-year-old son, with worry in his expression. "Sally said he went in searching for us. Is that true?"

"Yes. When I didn't see you outside with the other tenants, I thought you all were still inside."

"Is he going to be okay?" Kip asked as he approached her. Sally followed right behind her son.

"The paramedic thinks so." She hoped Samuel was right.

"Mom, he's got to be." Kip's lower lip quivered. "I begged Sally to take us to the park."

"Honey, you didn't know what might happen." She needed to listen to her own words, but that wasn't as easy as it sounded. "Let's get you two to Nana's, and then I'll go back to the hospital and check on him after the doctor has had time to see him in the E.R." Kathleen shifted toward her twenty-three-year-old cousin. "I'm so sorry about this, Sally. Do you want to go to Mom's?" She threw a glance toward the blaze. "It doesn't look like much will be left. You'll need a place to stay. You're welcome to stay with me and the boys."

"I appreciate the offer, but I can go to my mom's. I need to stay and talk with some of my neighbors. See what happened. Then I'll give Mom a call and have her come pick me up. She should be home. With Hurricane Naomi bearing down on us, I would have stayed at Mom's anyway." Sally looked south toward the water only a few blocks from the apartment building.

Kathleen couldn't think of that. The storm in the Gulf was still several days away from Hope, Mississippi, a quaint town of twenty thousand between Mobile and New Orleans. Her hometown of stately antebellum homes along the water thrived on tourism and the fishing industry. But anything could happen between now and the date the National Weather Service projected Naomi would come ashore in the vicinity of Hope.

"I called your cell earlier when I arrived. All I could do was leave a message."

Sally dug into her jean pocket and withdrew her phone. She winced. "Sorry. I had the sound off." Her cousin peered off to Kathleen's side. "Will Kip and Jared be okay?"

Kathleen followed the direction of Sally's attention. Both of her sons' gazes were glued to the commotion taking place at the Magnolia Street Apartments. Kip chewed his lower lip while her younger son took several feet forward. "I'd better get them away before Jared is in the middle of the chaos. I'll talk to you later. If you need any help, please call." She hugged her cousin, then made her way to her children, who were entranced by the plume of smoke bellowing into the sky being chased by yellow-orange flames.

Her mother would watch them while she went to check on the firefighter. She owed him that much for what he did for her. Kathleen clasped first Jared's hand, then Kip's. "We need to go to Nana's."

"But, Mom, I want to see what happens." He had told her on a number of occasions he wanted to be a firefighter.

"No. They don't need any more people here watching." Kathleen scanned the crowd that had gathered across the street from the apartments. "Besides, if Nana hears about this, she'll get worried."

"Will she even be back from Biloxi yet?" Kip trudged toward her car parked several buildings away.

"I hope so." Because she needed to go to the hospital. The firefighter had to be all right.

Will he make it?

The question plagued Kathleen the whole way into the E.R. thirty minutes later after she'd left her mother's house. Luckily her mother had returned from her weekly visit to her friend in a nursing home in Biloxi. Activity and tension met Kathleen as she came through the double doors. Ashley, an E.R. nurse who had befriended her when she'd begun working at Hope Memorial six weeks ago, hurried from behind the counter, saw her and came toward her.

"Thank the Lord you are here. We need a hand. One of the nurses got sick and had to go home. Can you help me with a patient? I have two that need attention." Ashley held up several vials of medicines and an IV bag.

"Is one of them the firefighter from the fire on Magnolia Street?" She rushed behind the counter and disposed of her purse in a drawer.

"Yes, he's in room two."

"I'll take him. I just came from the fire. My cousin lives in those apartments. I wanted to check to see how he is."

"I think he'll be all right. I haven't had much time with him yet. Besides him, there was a wreck on Interstate 10. Three injuries. It's been hopping around here. I don't want to even think about how it will be if Naomi hits here."

Neither did Kathleen. As a child, she had gone through two minor hurricanes that had gotten her out of school for a couple of days but, other than that, hadn't changed her life much at all. But Naomi was gathering speed and her winds were increasing.

Ashley thrust an IV bag into her hands. "He needs this."

Her breath caught in her throat, Kathleen took

it and started for the second door on the left. "What are his injuries?"

Ashley slanted a look at Kathleen and said, "I think several broken or cracked ribs, possible internal bleeding and smoke inhalation," then entered E.R. unit number four.

When Kathleen went into room two, she stared at the firefighter lying on the bed. His damp black hair was plastered against his head, and there were dark smudges on his tan face. His steely gray eyes locked on her and seized her full attention.

"Pete. What about Pete? Did my partner get out okay?" His raspy voice weakened with each word he uttered.

"Yes, there were no other injuries at the fire." Guilt swamped her at seeing the man she'd sent into the fire hurting, pain reflected in his gaze. The feeling was familiar. Hadn't her husband, Derek, blamed her for causing his stress that led to his heart attack? Shaking away the memory, Kathleen hung an IV drip on the pole and hooked up his line.

"I'll be fine." The firefighter struggled to sit up. His eyes clouded, his face twisting into a frown.

Kathleen rushed forward to restrain the patient's movements. "You need to lie down."

"You're the lady with the boys. Ruth's daughter." He swung one leg to the floor.

"Yes." Kathleen touched his left arm to stop him.

He flinched but proceeded with putting his other leg on the tiles, pushing himself upright. With a moan, he sank to the floor. Kathleen caught him as he went down and lessened his impact with the tiles. Kneeling next to him, she supported his back with her arm.

His head rested against the bottom of the bed. He fixed his weary gaze on her, pain dominating it. "I guess I'm not all right."

"Let's get you back in bed. The doctor will be here soon."

"Yeah, sure." His eyes fluttered and closed.

With her attention fastened on his face, Kathleen settled him on the floor and pressed the emergency call button.

"I thought you left here a couple of hours ago," Mildred Wyman, the floor supervisor, said as Kathleen exited the elevator and walked toward the nurses' station.

"I did, but there was a fire at the Magnolia Street Apartments where my cousin lives." She filled her in on the details. "When I came back to the hospital, Ashley recruited me to help until another nurse was able to come in. She just arrived so I wanted to see if Gideon O'Brien was settled into his room before I go home for sure this time."

"He's in room 345. He was asleep a little while ago."

"I'll peek in. See if he's up. If he needs anything."

Kathleen strolled toward the last room on the west wing's third floor. The memory of the look on Gideon O'Brien's face wouldn't leave her thoughts. Clearly he'd been in pain but he tried to deny the seriousness of his injuries. If only she had known that Sally had taken the boys to the park, Gideon O'Brien wouldn't be hurt.

She rapped on the door. When she didn't hear anything, she inched it open to see if he was still asleep. The dimly lit room beckoned her. She stepped inside and found him, lying on his bed, his head lolled to the side, his eyes closed.

With the black smudges cleaned from his face, his features fit together into a pleasing picture. High cheekbones, the beginnings of a dark stubble, strong jaw. His features drew her forward until she stood by his side, watching him sleep. She could remember seeing him a couple of times jogging past her mother's house when she had visited. When she'd told her mother who the injured firefighter was, her mom had said Gideon O'Brien had moved in down the street several years before.

"He sure is a handsome lad. Single, too." Her mother's words came back to taunt Kathleen. Before she'd had time to say goodbye to her sons so she could return to the hospital, her mother had ushered her out the door without further questions—which was unusual for her mom. Kathleen knew what was going through her mother's mind. A nice young man would solve all of Kathleen's problems. She would discourage her mother of that thought when she went back to pick up her sons.

Her glance ran down Gideon's length, categorizing his injuries. Two cracked ribs, wrapped but very painful, a broken arm above his left wrist, which would be set tomorrow, and an assortment of bruises. The doctor was still concerned about internal bleeding and wanted to keep a close eye on him overnight.

When her survey returned to his face, it connected with his gaze. Molten silver, framed by long, thick black eyelashes. Captivating. Powerful. Those thoughts sent warmth to her cheeks that she was sure rivaled the fire he'd fought.

Kathleen looked away. "I didn't mean to wake you up."

"You didn't," Gideon said in a scratchy voice. "You were at the fire. In the E.R. Ruth's daughter."

She nodded. "I'm so sorry you and Pete went

into the building after my children." She reconnected with him visually. "They were supposed to be there. I had come to pick them up. I didn't know Sally had taken them to the park and was running late getting them back to her apartment."

He shifted, gritting his teeth. "I'm glad they're safe."

"But—"

"So why are you up here?"

She wanted to say so much more to him, but a closed expression descended over his pain-filled features. "I wanted to make sure you were all right before I left."

"Define all right." One corner of his mouth lifted for a second then fell back into a neutral line. He tried to reach for the plastic cup of water on his nightstand and winced.

"Let me get it for you." Kathleen picked up the cup and held it to his lips so he could take a few sips. The scent of smoke clung to his dark hair. "Is your pain manageable?"

"I've had worse."

"You have?" She'd heard from other patients in the past how much broken or cracked ribs could hurt.

"Afraid so." Creases in his forehead deepened. Gideon gulped in a breath of air and started coughing. Agony contorted his features, his eyes shiny. "That hurt."

"Let me see if you can have more pain meds." Anything to help make him feel better. Then maybe she wouldn't feel so guilty.

He coughed again. His pale face urged her to hurry. She left his room and hastened to the nurses' station. "Mildred, can Gideon O'Brien have any more of his pain medication?"

"I'll check and take care of it. I was just coming to get you. Your mother called and said you need to get home right away. Something about Jared falling off the side of the house."

"Is he okay?"

"She didn't say. But she sounded shook up."

Kathleen rushed to the elevator, punching the down button. Seconds ticked by so slowly she started for the stairs when the doors swished open. This day was quickly going from bad to worse.

Two minutes later, after retrieving her purse in the E.R., she hastened out to the parking lot while digging for her cell. She slipped behind the steering wheel of her eight-year-old Dodge and punched in her mom's number.

"How's Jared?" In the background Kathleen heard her son crying, and her grip tightened on the phone.

"I don't know. He's holding his arm. He might have broken it."

"I'll be there soon." She flipped her cell closed and pulled out of the parking space.

Ten minutes later Kathleen turned onto Ocean-view Drive. Her seven-year-old son was too adventurous for his own good. She guessed he was going from climbing trees to houses now. Next he'd want to try flying off the roof. The thought sent panic through her as she drove into the drive-way and parked.

The front door banged open, and Kip came racing out of the two-story stone house. "Mom, Jared climbed up there." He pointed toward the second floor. "You should have seen him. I can't believe he did it."

"Did you dare him?" Kathleen charged up the steps to the porch. At the door Kip's silence prompted her to glance back at him. "You did."

"Aw, Mom. I didn't think he would really do it."

"We'll talk later." Kathleen entered her child-hood home and headed toward the kitchen where the crying was coming from.

Kathleen's mother stood over her son, her face leached of color. "I'm so glad you're here." Relief flooded her features. "If you need me, I'll be—"

"Mom, I'll take care of this. Don't worry." Her mom never did well when someone was hurt or even sick. She usually fell apart. She certainly hadn't gotten her desire to be a nurse from her mother.

Jared sat cross-legged on the tile floor, cradling his left arm to his chest, tears streaking down his face. His look whisked away any anger she had at him attempting something dangerous.

Kathleen stooped down, putting her hand on his shoulder. "Honey, where does it hurt?"

He sniffled. "Here." He lifted his arm and pointed at his wrist. "Nana thinks I broke it."

When Kathleen gently probed his injury, Jared yelped and tried to pull away.

"Let's take you to the doctor. You'll need an X-ray."

"Am I gonna get a shot?" Jared's brown eyes grew round and large.

"I don't know."

"I am! I don't want to go." Jared scooted back from her. "I can tough it out."

"If it's broken, it needs to be fixed. It'll hurt a lot more than a shot if you don't get it taken care of."

"Don't be a baby," Kip said behind Kathleen.

She threw a warning look over her shoulder. "I'm sure you have homework. Go do it. Have Nana help you if you need it."

Jared stopped moving away from her. He peered down at his wrist, sniffed and then locked gazes with her. "I'm not a baby." He pushed to his feet, tears swimming in his eyes. Blinking, he ran his right hand across his face, scrubbing away the evidence of his crying. "I'm ready," he announced as if he were being led away to some horrible fate.

While Jared trudged toward the front door, Kathleen spied Kip sitting on the stairs. Before her older son could open his mouth, she followed Jared into the foyer. Jared went outside on the porch, sticking his tongue out at his brother as he left.

Kathleen swept around, her hand resting on her waist. "Don't forget you and I need to have a talk. This fighting between you two has got to stop."

"We don't fight."

She arched her eyebrow. "Oh, since when?"

"We're playing."

Gesturing toward the den, she said, "Homework. I want to see it finished by the time I get back to Nana's to pick you up."

Kip leaped to his feet and stomped toward the den, making enough racket to wake up anyone who was within a several house radius.

As Kathleen covered the distance to the den to tell her mother what she was going to do, her mom said, "Glory be. This is great news."

Kathleen stepped through the entrance into the room. "What is?" she asked, swinging her attention to The Weather Channel on TV. She could certainly use some good news.

Her mom muted the announcer. "Hurricane Naomi has changed course. I think we're going to miss most of it. Maybe get a touch of the western tip, but not like they had predicted."

"We don't have to board up our house now?" Kip sat down at the gaming table with his book bag.

"It's not looking like we do." Her mom peered at her. "I know it's not good news for someone else, but maybe it will peter out before it reaches Florida."

Kathleen doubted it from the information she had heard. "Mom, I'm taking Jared to the minor emergency clinic. I don't know when I'll be back to pick up Kip."

"Fine. Kip and I will put away all the supplies I bought for the hurricane, especially all those boxes of tape I got for the windows, which I really don't need. Don't know why I bought them."

"I'll take a box, Nana," Kip announced while digging into his bag for his homework.

"Sure. Just don't tape up Jared with it." Her mother rose and moved toward Kip. "Kathleen, when you get back we'll order something for dinner. We're celebrating tonight. No Naomi."

Kathleen left her mom's, not feeling the least bit in the mood to celebrate anything—even the fact the town would avoid Naomi. Her cousin's apartment burned today. She could have lost Sally and her sons. A firefighter went into a burning building because of her insistence her family was still inside.

Her life continued to come apart at the seams, starting with the last year of her marriage to Derek. She had wanted coming home to be a new start but hadn't counted on her sons' rebellion against moving to Hope. There was no going back to Denver, however. She couldn't afford to live there, financially or emotionally.

Chapter Two

The crashing sounds of the falling timbers and the crackling of the fire haunted Gideon when he tried to sleep at the hospital. He remembered being put into the ambulance and glancing at the Magnolia Street Apartments as the structure caved in on itself, flames shooting upward as the blaze rampaged through it.

The noises around him amplified in volume. The antiseptic smell of the hospital overwhelmed him. Sweat popped out on his forehead. His breathing became shallow, his throat raw.

Finally, Gideon inhaled a deeper breath and regretted it the second he did. A sharp pain pierced through his chest. He clenched his jaw and rode the wave until it subsided to a throbbing ache. In spite of how he felt, restlessness churned through him. Scanning the hospital room, he resisted the impulse to walk away. The doctor should be here within a few hours to give him the okay to leave. But as he stared at the clock on the wall across from his bed, the second hand seemed to be moving in slow motion.

The sound of the door opening lured his attention away from watching time inch forward. Kathleen Hart—last night he'd finally remembered she'd told him her name at the fire—entered his room. Her long blond hair pulled back in a ponytail emphasized her delicate features— large, blue eyes like the Gulf off the shores of Hope, lips with a rosy tint that wasn't from lipstick, and two dimples in her cheeks as she smiled at him.

Dressed in blue scrubs, she approached his bed carrying a little plastic cup with his meds. "How are you doing today?"

"Well enough to go home." He held out his right palm for his pills.

"Dr. Adams should be here soon. He does rounds after lunch." Dark shadows under her eyes attested to not enough rest.

He recalled her apology and hoped what had happened at the fire hadn't caused her a sleepless night. "Where did you go yesterday? Nurse Ratched brought me my meds. She wouldn't tell me what happened to you."

"I won't tell Mildred you called her that."

He grinned. "She's definitely a no-nonsense nurse. I'm glad you came back today."

"I work on this floor. I had to."

"Ouch. I think my ego was just wounded."

"Only think?" A twinkle danced briefly in her tired eyes.

The shadow in her gaze tugged at him. He wanted to prolong the light tone of the conversation, but he needed her to understand how he felt. His injuries weren't her fault. "You were upset yesterday. Are you all right today?"

"The more important question is, are you?"

"I will be in time."

"You shouldn't be here right now. If only I had waited a little..." Her voice faded into silence, and she glanced away, swallowing hard.

"I would rather err on the side of caution than have someone trapped in a burning building. What I did yesterday is part of my job. Occasionally we go into a fire looking for a person who isn't there. It happens. You are *not* to blame." He would never forget the firefighters who had rescued him and his younger brother from a fire when he was eight. If they hadn't come into his burning house, he and Zach wouldn't be alive today. "No more guilt over yesterday. I'm glad your sons are safe."

With her gaze still averted, she nodded.

He wasn't totally convinced she wasn't blaming

herself anymore, not if the furrowed forehead and the darkening of the blue in her eyes were any indication. "I've been hurt before. I won't let a few cracked ribs and a broken arm get me down."

She swiveled her attention back to him, her expression evening out, but the dark circles under her eyes were still there. "Tell that to my son. He broke a bone in his wrist yesterday after I took him to his grandmother's while I came to the hospital. That's where I had to go. He told me at the doctor's office that he wanted to see the hurricane coming in the Gulf. He thought the view would be better from the roof."

"I heard it turned toward Florida. We might get some high tides and rain, but hopefully that will be all." He shifted in the bed and caused another shaft of pain to constrict his breath, but he tried to keep from flinching. He didn't succeed.

"Are you all right?" The wrinkled forehead returned with a slight tensing.

"Just a twinge. Nothing that won't go away with time. So how did he get to the roof? Ladder?"

"That would have been safer. But he climbed the side of the house on a dare from his older brother. He didn't make it. He fell while trying to hoist himself onto the roof."

Gideon whistled. "You've got a daredevil on your hands. What did your husband say about it?" The second he asked the question he wanted to snatch it back. He didn't see a wedding ring on her left hand, but there was paler skin where one would have been. He couldn't remember Ruth saying anything to him about her son-in-law, but then he and Ruth were only passing acquaintances on Oceanview Drive.

"Derek died last year."

"I'm so sorry. I…" He didn't know what else to say.

"Is there anything I can do for you before I leave?" A professional facade fell into place as she checked his IV drip.

He could respect that she wanted to shut down the subject of her husband. Losing a loved one was difficult. Although he had never been married, he'd lost too many people in his life not to feel a kinship with her.

He grinned, wanting to see the light back in her eyes. "Other than get me out of here, no."

"Sorry, but Dr. Adams might take exception to that. Just as soon as he signs your discharge papers, you can escape."

"A hospital isn't my favorite place." Again he was reminded of his parents' deaths. His father had died in the fire, but his mother with third degree burns had lingered for a day in the hospital. He had only been able to say goodbye to her at the end when she was unconscious. He would never forget that last time he saw her.

"It usually isn't for most people." Her smile reappeared on her face, a sparkle shining in her eyes—making him forget where he was for a moment. "If you need anything, use your call button."

He watched her saunter out of his room. Occasionally he and Ruth would talk when they saw each other on the street, but with his crazy schedule, it wasn't often. She had mentioned she had only one child, and then this August she had talked about her daughter returning home in September to live in Hope. Other than Ruth being excited her two grandsons would be close, she hadn't gone into details about the move.

From his and Kathleen's few exchanges, he had sensed a deep hurt and now that he knew about her husband dying, he figured that must be why. One more reason he didn't get too involved in people's lives. He found after being shuffled between one foster family and another that it was safer to stay emotionally apart from others. Much safer.

After passing out the medication to her patients, Kathleen came back to the nurses' station to write in their charts. Dr. Adams nodded to her as he headed down the hall toward Gideon's room. She smiled, thinking about how the man would finally be able to leave. Even with his injuries, he had exuded restlessness. When he had told her about a hospital not being one of his favorite places, she'd heard pain behind the words though he'd no doubt tried to hide it.

Although he had reassured her she wasn't at fault for his being hurt, she had been married to a man who had blamed her for all his woes. Even with some of his last words to her right before he slipped away after having a massive heart attack at the age of thirty-five, he'd blamed her for the stress he'd lived under. No matter how much she told herself that she hadn't wanted him to take all the money out of their savings for Kip and Jared's college fund to invest in the stock market in risky companies, it didn't ease the guilt. In fact, she hadn't even known about it until after his death. The stocks hadn't done what her husband had dreamed they would. In fact, when he'd had his heart attack, she had discovered Derek had put the family thirty thousand dollars into debt and just that day had gotten notification the bank was foreclosing on their house if the mortgage wasn't paid. She'd tried to do that, but it hadn't been enough.

She shook the past from her mind. Coming to Hope was a fresh start, even if she still had twenty-eight thousand dollars to pay back. When she had lived here, she had flourished in the small-town feel and kindness of others. She desperately needed that now.

An orderly went by her desk and entered Gideon's room. Not long after that she saw Gideon appear in the hallway, dressed to leave, sitting in a wheelchair.

At the nurses' station he had the orderly stop. "Thank everyone for me for their excellent but *brief* care," he told her with a smile.

"I see Nate is helping break you out of here."

"Yep. I was getting ready to walk out of the hospital when he showed up."

"Oh, we cannot have that. Against Hope Memorial's policy," she said in dead seriousness, but the second the words came out she chuckled. "You aren't the first who has threatened that."

He motioned her to bend down closer to him, then he whispered, "Now my only complaint is that I would have liked a prettier escort. Too bad you're busy." Gideon winked and flashed her a grin before the orderly wheeled him toward the elevator.

Kathleen touched her cheek. It felt hot beneath her fingertips. She hadn't blushed in years and this was the second time since meeting Gideon. The injured firefighter was charming, but that was all he was. She didn't have the emotional energy to get involved with anyone, even if she felt guilty for his injuries. Raising her sons and slowly paying off the mountain of bills her husband had left her were enough to deal with.

Her mother kept telling her to turn it over to the Lord. She used to, but in the past two years she hadn't seen any evidence of the Lord in her life. Her prayers for help had gone unanswered. She was still in debt. Her sons desperately needed a man's influence. They hated being in Hope. They fought all the time. Then to top it all off, she felt responsible for Gideon's injuries, no matter what he said.

Which means I'll make sure he's comfortable while he's recuperating at home. That's the least I can do. Then maybe I won't feel so bad when I see him in a cast and wincing from pain.

Kathleen came into the house by the back door, thankful that her car had made it at least to her mom's, although she'd had doubts several blocks away when it died on her yet again. After the third time cranking the engine, it turned over and started.

Her mother told her to use her kitchen to make Gideon something to eat, then she could just walk down a few houses and give it to him. This was something Kathleen could do for him. She'd grown up with neighbors helping neighbors. That was part of Hope's charm. With one arm in the cast it would be hard for Gideon at first learning to do things one-handed. He didn't need to worry about making something to eat.

Kathleen set the bag of food she'd gotten to make her Mexican chicken dish on the counter. After emptying the sack, she placed the pieces of chicken in water to cook. Then she went in search of her sons to see what kind of homework they had. When her mother didn't go see her friend in Biloxi, she watched Jared and Kip after school until Kathleen got off work and could pick them up. And when her mother couldn't watch her sons, Sally would fill in, no charge. That was a huge help to her because she couldn't afford to pay childcare along with everything else to raise two growing boys.

"Mom, do you know where Jared and Kip are?" Kathleen asked when she entered the den where her mother was watching The Weather Channel.

She peered toward Kathleen. "I didn't hear you come in. Been glued to the T.V. I'm charting the progress of Naomi even if it is going to miss us."

Kathleen wasn't surprised by that fact. Her mom had done that for years. She had a stack of charts of past hurricanes that had come into the Gulf. "I'm going to fix some Mexican chicken for us and take some to Gideon O'Brien down the street like I mentioned to you."

"I'm sure he'll enjoy that. He seems quite lonely to me."

Before her mother had her fixed up on a date with Gideon, Kathleen asked, "Where are the boys? They need to get their homework done. After dinner they are useless. I can't get much out of them then as far as schoolwork."

"They said something about riding those old bikes I had in the garage. I told them they could but not to go farther than this block and not to ride in the streets."

Kathleen glimpsed the time on the clock above the mantel. "It's getting late. I'd better round them up and see where they stand with their homework."

"We'll need to pray for the people in Panama City." Her mother listened to the reporter on the T.V. give the latest coordinates of the hurricane and jotted them down. "I'm sure you'll see the boys if you go outside and look."

That was assuming her sons obeyed their grandmother when she babysat them. Lately there was no guarantee they would. Kathleen made her way toward the front door. Outside on the lawn she looked to the left and saw no one. Then she peered toward the right and thought she saw a bike that was like the one she'd ridden as a child lying on the sidewalk three houses down where Gideon lived.

She remembered Kip's questions the night before about the firefighter who had been hurt in the Magnolia Street Apartments fire. He had wanted to know if he would be all right. Who was he? Could he and Jared make get-well cards for him? She'd kissed her boys good-night and told them she would talk to them today when she got home from work.

She charged down the street. Knowing them, they had taken matters into their own hands without waiting to discuss it with her.

At Gideon's one-story white house with a neat yard, she skirted around both of her mom's old bikes and headed straight for the front door. After ringing the bell, she waited, trying to temper her anger that Kip and Jared would disturb a man recovering from some painful injuries.

Her older son opened the door. "Hey, Mom. Come in."

"No, I think you all have stayed long enough. You and Jared need to come back to Nana's. You're both supposed to have your homework finished by dinner." *Haven't we done enough to disrupt this man's life?*

"Aw, Mom, Gideon was telling us about some of the rescues he's done."

"Why are you answering his door?" She swung open the screen, the one standing between her and Kip.

"Gideon doesn't move too fast. I told him I'd get it."

Kathleen glanced over her son's shoulder at the slow-moving firefighter making his way toward them with a small white dog with a curly tail. His stiff movements coupled with the sight of his cast only reinforced why the man was in the pain he was.

"Hello, Kathleen. Your sons came over to give me their get-well cards. I asked them to stay if it was okay with you. They assured me it was." Gideon's gaze swept from Kip to Jared, who had joined them in the foyer.

Her younger son poked his head around Gideon. "He has a cast just like me. Isn't that neat? We're twins."

"And that is Butch. He's so sweet," Kip added, pointing to the dog near Gideon.

"It's time for you two to come back to Nana's and get your homework done."

"Mooomm, can't we stay for a while longer?" Kip's mouth formed his classic pout that he had stood in front of the mirror one day to perfect.

"Another time, guys. This is a school night, and you've got work to do." Gideon tousled Jared's, then Kip's hair.

Jared giggled then scooted out the front door.

But Kip remained where he was standing. "Will you tell us some more stories about being a firefighter?"

"Well, sure, anytime it's all right with your mother." Gideon flashed her a grin that melted any irritation she had toward her sons for bothering the man.

"Great. Call if you need us to do anything for you. After school we stay with Nana until Mom comes to pick us up." Kip raced past Kathleen and stamped down the porch steps.

While her sons grabbed their bikes and rode them toward her mother's house, Kathleen faced Gideon. "I know how tired you must be. Your body has gone through a trauma and needs rest, not my sons bothering you. I'm sorry—"

He held up his palm to still her words. "I enjoyed their visit. I was resting on the couch, getting more bored by the second when they came and rescued me from my boredom. I hope you'll let them come again."

She completely surrendered to the kindness in his eyes. Her legs grew weak, and she clutched the door frame to steady herself. "Only as long as they don't pester you." The pale cast to his skin spoke of the strain of standing. "Let me help you back to that couch."

He shook his head. "As much as I'd like a pretty lady to hold me, I can make my own way there."

"Are you sure?"

"Yes. Do you need to watch to make sure I don't falter halfway there?"

She grinned. "I'll take your word for it. Besides, I need to get home and make you a dinner, which I plan to bring you if that's okay with you."

"Normally I would jump at the chance to have someone fix me dinner, but you should see my refrigerator. There is nothing like good ole Southern hospitality. I don't think I'll be able to eat half the dishes stuffed in it. The ladies at my church decided they would stock it for me, so I wouldn't have to worry about what to eat for the next week. Well, more like several."

"Then I'll wait until later when you've run out of their dishes. I know it takes a while for ribs to heal, and they can be painful."

"Like I said, I don't usually turn down a home-cooked meal, so you'll get no argument from me. When it's my time to cook at the fire station, I've actually heard some groans from the other firefighters."

She chuckled. "If you need anything, I only live two blocks away. Down the hill and around the corner."

"On Bayview Avenue?"

"Yeah, the yellow cottage. One of Mom's rentals. Good night." Which was the main reason she could save a little money to pay off her debt. Her mother didn't charge her rent, but Kathleen had insisted on paying all the utilities and other bills connected to the house.

He stood in his doorway with his dog next to him as she descended the porch steps. She felt his gaze on her the whole way down his sidewalk. Heat flared into her cheeks. She couldn't resist glancing over her shoulder, only to find him staring at her, as she thought. He nodded, then swung his door closed.

Kathleen hurried to the foyer to answer the door. When she opened it, her breath caught for a few seconds. Although she'd found herself thinking about Gideon several times since she'd seen him yesterday, she hadn't thought she would see him this soon. "This is a surprise. What brings you by here?"

He lifted two large pizza boxes. "I came bearing dinner. I couldn't stand staying in my home another moment. I immediately thought of you and your sons. You were kind to want to fix me dinner. I thought I would beat you to the punch. I called earlier to see if y'all would be home and Kip said yes. I asked him if you had started dinner. He said you had to run next door and were behind schedule." He handed her the boxes. "He was supposed to tell you I was bringing dinner."

"A minor detail he forgot. I wondered why he kept coming up with things I had to do before starting dinner. You didn't have to bring pizza. I owe you a dinner, not the other way around. Remember?"

"I'm not used to inactivity. It was a spur-of-the-moment decision. I figured the boys would like pizza."

She smiled. "Pizza and just about every other junk food there is." Stepping to the side, Kathleen opened the door wider. "Come on in."

As Gideon entered the house, one corner of his mouth hiked up. "I was hoping you wouldn't send me home with all this pizza."

"You may change your mind after being here a while." She started for the kitchen at the back of the house. "I should warn you. My sons have been fighting most of the day. At the moment they are in time-out. And we've only been home an hour."

"Sounds like a few boys I have in my youth group at church."

"Youth group?"

"I help out when I can with the group for eight- to twelve-year-olds. When I'm not working, we sometimes play a game or two of basketball in the evening at the park near the Hope Community Church. There are several courts there. By the time they go home, they're too exhausted to fight each other. A couple of the dads have joined our little games, too."

"Is that Broussard Park on the Point?"

"Yeah. I like to run there sometimes."

Memories intruded into her mind. Memories of happier times before her father had been killed in an accident at the shipyard. "When I was a child, my family used to go to the Point to watch the sun set and have a picnic dinner."

"Since I came here, I've seen some beautiful sunsets on the Point."

Kathleen went into the kitchen with Gideon following close behind her. After placing the boxes on the table, she peered over her shoulder at him. "Where are you from?"

"New Orleans, originally. I've been here for five years."

"How long have you been a firefighter?"

"Fifteen years."

"Why did you decide to become one?"

He opened his mouth but a few seconds later snapped it closed. A nerve in his jaw twitched. Clasping his hands so tightly his knuckles whitened, he stared straight ahead at a spot over her shoulder. "Someone needs to fight fires."

Behind what he'd said there was a wealth of words left unspoken, but his stiff posture and steely expression told her the subject was off-limits. What was really behind him being a firefighter? On the surface he seemed open and friendly, but deep down she felt his need for privacy as though he were used to being alone and liked it that way. She could respect his need for that.

She'd felt the same way when she'd discovered the extent of Derek's debt and betrayal after he died. Leaving her to deal with the aftermath. Alone. So yes, she was used to dealing with her problems alone.

For a long moment an uncomfortable silence vibrated in the air between them.

Gideon cleared his throat. "I've filled in as a paramedic when they've needed me. I'm surprised I haven't met you before at the hospital."

Covering the distance to the refrigerator, she took out a carton of milk and a pitcher of iced tea. "That's because I started working at Hope Memorial Hospital a little over six weeks ago. Knowing your aversion to a hospital, I doubt you hung around once you delivered your patients to the E.R."

"Ah, you know me too well. Where did you move from?"

"Denver, Colorado." Kathleen poured milk into two large glasses.

"Can I help you set the table or something?"

"No, I've got this. You brought the dinner. That's enough, and my sons will be ecstatic they aren't having what I planned tonight—tuna casserole."

"I ran into your mother as I was leaving my house. She asked me where I was going when I should be resting. I told her I was feeling better and decided to take dinner to you and the boys. She gave her stamp of approval."

I'm sure she did. Her mother was a romantic at heart and had encouraged Kathleen to start dating almost immediately after returning home. "She goes out every Thursday night with Mildred."

"Not Nurse Ratched?"

"The one and the same."

Gideon rubbed the back of his neck, his forehead creased. "She's a friend of the family?"

"Yes."

"That will teach me to keep my mouth shut."

"She comes across tough and no-nonsense, but she really has a very loving heart. That is, once you get to know her." Kathleen pressed her lips together to keep from smiling at the sheepish look on his face. "I tell you what. You can get the plates down from that cabinet and napkins from that drawer—" she pointed to the locations " and I'll go get the boys before this pizza gets cold."

As she strolled from the kitchen, the sensation

that he was staring at her sent a tingling wave through her. Goose bumps rose on her arms. She quickened her pace down the hallway to Jared and Kip's room. She'd had her younger son go into the bedroom the boys shared while Kip was in hers. Time-out in the same room only escalated their skirmishes, which had been growing worse since they'd moved to Hope.

When she opened the door to the boys' bedroom, Jared sat on his twin bed, chunking paper wads into the trashcan. A whole notebook, almost gone, littered the floor.

"Jared!"

He glanced at her, grinned and said, "Watch me, Mom." He tore the last sheet from the pad and scrunched it up into a ball, then tossed it toward the basket. It bounced off the rim and dropped into the pile of other missed shots. He frowned. "Maybe I should move it closer."

"No, maybe you should clean this mess up and then come to dinner. We're having pizza."

"Not tuna? Yay!" He scooted off the bed, taking half the covers with him. "The only reason I didn't make many baskets was cause I can't use both arms."

"Then I would refrain from climbing houses."

He bent over and picked up the first wad, frowning at his cast on his left arm. "This is gonna take forever."

"You should have thought about that before you decided to make the mess." She turned away before he saw her smile. Natural consequences were great teachers, but her son could have broken something much worse than his wrist.

Across the hall, she found Kip at the door listening to her and Jared. She peeked into her room to make sure he hadn't left a similar mess.

He looked up at her with those big brown eyes and long eyelashes and said sweetly, "I'm sorry I fought with Jared, but he was bugging me. I had to do something to shut him up."

"Getting into a wrestling match isn't an option. Dinner is ready."

"I heard the doorbell. Did Gideon come with pizzas?"

"Yes."

"Sweet." Kip hurried ahead of her toward the kitchen.

"Next time, young man, warn me when someone is coming over, especially with dinner."

Jared came out of his room and followed behind Kathleen. "Why did he bring pizza?"

Kathleen waited for Jared, cradling his cast to his chest. "To see you all."

"Really? Us?"

"I think he enjoyed your visit yesterday. He thought you and Kip might enjoy pizza."

"Kip talked his ear off. I hardly got to say anything. He was constantly asking him about what a firefighter did."

When she and Jared entered the kitchen, Kip was already seated at his place with three pieces of pizza with all the toppings on it. "I'm starved, Mom."

"We're coming." Her gaze latched on to Gideon standing by the counter. She crossed to the table and took a seat. Gideon moved behind her and helped her scoot her chair forward before he sat. She couldn't remember the last time a man had done that for her.

After Jared plopped down in the last place between Gideon and Kip, Gideon looked at each boy. "I remember Kip mentioning how much he loved pizza yesterday. Earlier that sounded good to me, so I thought I would share some with y'all."

"Pizza is okay." Jared dug into the box nearest him and pulled out four pieces, piling them on his plate.

"Hold it. You never eat that many." Kathleen clasped her hands into fists in her lap. "Take one at a time."

"Kip has three pieces," Jared whined.

"The same goes for him, too." Kathleen pinned her older son with a stare that told him to behave.

"Sorry." Kip began to put his slices back.

"Leave them. You've already put them on your

plate, but next time one piece at a time. I expect you two to eat every last bite of what you have on your plate." *Lord, give me patience.* "Remember your manners. We have a guest tonight."

Both of her sons hung their heads but exchanged narrow-eyed glances.

"Jared, it's your turn to say the blessing." Kathleen uncurled her hands.

"Bless this food. Amen." Jared jerked up his head, grabbed his first piece and took a big bite.

When Gideon reached for a slice of Canadian Bacon, her favorite, Jared's gaze fixed on his cast on his left arm that came down to his wrist but allowed him the use of his hand.

"No one has signed your cast," he said with a full mouth of food. Kathleen gave him *the look,* and Jared immediately chewed his pizza and swallowed before adding, "I've got most of my friends to sign mine at school. Annie wanted to, but I wouldn't let her." He held up his arm as though he had a trophy in his grasp.

"Why not?" Gideon poured some iced tea into his glass.

"A girl? No way. I would never hear the end of it." Jared's mouth pinched together, and he tilted his head in a thoughtful look. "Can you work with that cast? I'm having trouble doing things with mine."

A fleeting frown flitted across Gideon's features. "Not where I want to be. I'll be stuck behind a desk at headquarters until this comes off."

"I have to wear mine for six weeks. How about you?"

"Seven or eight weeks."

"Bummer," Kip said, pulling Gideon's attention to him. "That sounds boring."

"Yep. But I'm not much use to the team with only one arm fully functioning. That's why it's important to be as careful as you can, so you don't end up in a situation like this." Gideon tapped his cast. "Not fun."

"Can I sign your cast? I want to be the first." Kip jumped up and headed for the desk to retrieve a red marker.

"Sure. I noticed it was a little bare after seeing yours, Jared."

"Can I sign yours, too? I'll let you do mine."

Kathleen relaxed back against the chair while the boys wrote their names on Gideon's cast. As he searched Jared's cast for a blank space to put his signature, her throat tightened. Lately her two sons hadn't done anything together without launching into a fight. When Kip finally spotted a place for Gideon to scribble his name, Kathleen lowered her head and blinked away the moisture in her eyes. How could she let something as simple as this get to her?

Chapter Three

Later that evening, with darkness beyond the porch light, Kathleen drew in a deep breath of the cool air with a salty tang to it. The Gulf of Mexico was one block away. She could almost hear the waves crashing against the shore. When she got a chance, she loved to run on the beach early in the morning before the town woke up. It had become her haven since she'd come back to Hope.

Still in her scrubs from work, she rubbed her hands up and down her arms. "It's starting to finally feel like fall some. I'd gotten used to having four seasons in Colorado."

Gideon came up behind her and leaned back on the railing. "I'm going to hate seeing October end next week. It's one of my favorite months. In the middle of football season. Not as oppressively hot as in the summer. But I'll take that over cold weather any day. I'm a New Orleans native—hot and muggy is what I'm used to."

"Jared and Kip won't like the fact it rarely snows here. When I was growing up in Hope, it only did once. An inch. Shut down the whole town for a day until it melted."

"Do they know that?"

"I'm not telling them."

The sound of his chuckle filled the space between them, warming Kathleen. His gaze roamed over her features and for a few seconds wiped all thoughts from her mind, except the man who had shared a dinner with them and entertained her sons with stories about his job. Kip had hung on every word Gideon had said. Even Jared had listened until he couldn't sit still any longer. He'd lasted fifteen minutes, five minutes longer than usual.

"Thanks for bringing the pizzas over. You're a big hit with my sons."

"They're good kids."

She opened her mouth to agree with him when she heard a scream then, "Mom!"

She rushed into the house and hurried down the hallway, Gideon right behind her. Past calamities caused by her sons zipped through her thoughts. Jared ran out of his bedroom with Kip on his heels. Her older son tackled his brother to the floor.

"You're dead meat. How many times do I have to tell you not to touch my stuff?" Kip sat on Jared's chest, pinning his brother's arms to the carpet with his knees. He raised his hands and balled them.

"Kip, get off Jared."

Kip flashed her a scowl, his fists still hovering over Jared's face. "He tore up my notebook. I had my homework in it for school tomorrow."

Kathleen settled her hand on Kip's shoulder. "I'll take it from here."

"But, Mom, I've got to do my homework over. It's all torn up. It was hard. I hate math, and now I've got to figure it all out again."

Gideon stepped into Kip's line of vision. "You know I'm pretty good with math. I'll help you while your mom and Jared have a talk."

Kip's eyes grew round. "You will?"

Gideon nodded.

"I'll get my book. There's paper in the desk in the kitchen." Kip bounced once on his brother's stomach, which produced a grunt from Jared, then stood.

Scrambling to his feet, Jared grimaced, holding his middle. "Mom, did you see him? He hurt me. On purpose."

Kathleen waited to answer him until Kip and Gideon disappeared down the hallway, then she whirled to face Jared. "You used your brother's school notebook to make paper wads?"

He suddenly found a spot on the floor by his feet extremely interesting. Scuffing his tennis shoe against the carpet, he murmured, "He hadn't finished his homework. He only had four problems done. He'd told Nana he had done more than he had after school."

"That's not the point. You have to respect your brother's things."

Jared lifted his head. "I want my own room like I had in Colorado. I hate sharing with him. He's always bothering my stuff. He always has to be first. He always has to have the last word."

"That isn't going to happen anytime soon."

"Why did we move here? I hate this place. I miss my friends." Tears glistening in his eyes, he curled his fingers into tight balls, his face screwed up into a frown.

"I had to sell our house in Colorado. We needed a place to live. I grew up here, and I thought you all would enjoy it like I did."

The frown deepened into a scowl. "You're a girl. All my friends are back home. Not here."

"You've got friends. How about Charlie down the street? How about the kids who signed your cast?"

A teardrop shone on his eyelash then rolled down his cheek. He knuckled it away. "It's not the same." He spun on his heel and raced into his room, throwing himself on his bed and burying his face in his pillow.

After entering, Kathleen sat next to her son and laid her hand on his arm. "Honey, I know this house is small, but it's all I can afford. One day we'll get to move to a bigger place."

Jared popped back up, his eyes flaring wide in hope. "Back home?"

"No. We're staying in Hope. I need my family around me."

"They can come visit. I'll even let Nana have my room when she does and share with Kip."

"Honey, that's not possible."

Jared turned his back on her and hugged his pillow to his chest. "You don't care about what I want. We were fine where we were."

Coming to Hope hadn't been an easy decision. She'd hated asking for help, but she'd had no choice. She'd needed a support system and a means to save money to pay off the debts. "I'll always care, but we had to move. The cost of living was too high in Colorado."

Still facing away from her, he murmured, "Cost of living?"

"How much it takes to pay for things you need."

"I don't have to have ice cream, and you can forget I want a new bike for Christmas. The one at Nana's is just fine, even if it's a girl's." He twisted toward her. "And I can wear Kip's clothes when he can't anymore. Can we move back?"

"As much as I appreciate your offers, we still can't move back to Denver. This is our home now."

The frown returned, and he faced away from her. "You never listen to me. Only Kip."

"One day you'll understand there are some things that can't be changed no matter how much you want otherwise." Something she had learned painfully the past couple of years. She sat for a few more minutes, but when Jared didn't say anything else, she pushed to her feet. "You need to apologize to your brother. If you bother his things anymore, you'll be grounded next time. Understand?"

"Yeah, you love him more than me."

She leaned over and kissed the side of his head. "I love you both the same. Don't forget to tell your brother you're sorry."

Jared scrubbed her kiss away and put his pillow over his head.

Kathleen walked from the bedroom, releasing a long sigh. *Lord, I need help.*

With his tongue sticking out the side of his mouth, Kip wrote down the answer and waited to see if Gideon said it was right. When he did,

Kip beamed. "Thanks, Gideon, I think I get this long division now."

"I'm glad. I used to struggle with math until one year I had this teacher who I connected with. I finally understood what I was supposed to do. After that, math has come easy to me."

"I've only got one more problem. I've never done my homework this fast."

Gideon watched him finish his math sheet. When the hairs on his nape stood up, he knew that Kathleen had come into the kitchen. He felt her gaze on him and straightened his shoulders, resisting the urge to peer back at her. He dated women all the time, but none of them had caught his attention like she had.

Deep down he sensed a connection as if she knew what it was to be hurt deeply and had held herself back from others because of that. Like him. Was that why he'd gotten the bright idea to bring dinner to her tonight?

No, it was her sons. When he'd talked to them there was something that reminded him of his younger brother and him growing up in foster homes—until one day a family had adopted Zach, leaving Gideon alone. It was obvious she needed help with her sons, and for the next seven weeks or so, he would have more time on his hands than usual while he recovered from his injuries and finally could return to full duty.

He pivoted toward her, transfixed by the soft blue of her eyes. *Run.* The one word set off an alarm bell in his mind. His chest constricted.

"Is this right, Gideon?"

In the distance he heard Kip speaking to him, but Gideon couldn't tear his eyes from Kathleen, her delicate features forming a beautiful picture that could haunt him if he allowed her to get too close. But he wouldn't do that.

Run. Now.

He wrenched his gaze away and glanced down at the last problem. "Sure. You did great. I'd better be going. I imagine you need to go to bed early with school tomorrow, and I have a lot to do in the morning. I…" He clamped his jaws closed before he made a fool of himself with his ramblings.

"I'm going to show Gideon out, Kip. You stay in here. Do not go to your bedroom until I get back."

"Can I have some ice cream? I finished my homework, and it's all correct. Gideon said so."

"One small bowl."

As Kip jumped up and went to the refrigerator, Kathleen swung around and exited the kitchen.

"See you soon, sport. I'll see about that tour of the station." Gideon left and found Kathleen in the foyer, waiting for him. "I told Kip I'll arrange a tour of Station Two for him—for all of you. But only if you say it's okay."

"He wants to be a firefighter or a doctor. He hasn't made up his mind."

"I'd say he has a few years to do that. How about Jared?"

She shrugged. "He hasn't said anything. But the way he's going, I could see him being a test pilot or some other kind of job that is daring. Danger means nothing to him while I'm getting gray hairs at the young age of thirty-two."

"How about professional mountain climber?"

"Please don't mention that. Sides of houses are enough for me," she said with a laugh.

He liked seeing her two dimples appear in her cheeks when she laughed. Her eyes lit with a bright gleam that transformed her. "I enjoyed tonight. Of course, I'm not sure what I'm going to do until they allow me to work behind the desk at headquarters."

"Read a good book."

"I'm more an action kind of guy. Reading is too sedate for me. I tried today to circumvent procedures by reporting for desk duty and was told by the chief in no uncertain terms to stay away until I get the go-ahead from the doc. That should be in three days."

"Does that mean your ribs aren't hurting? That's quick."

"I didn't say that." As he stood in the foyer, his cracked ribs were protesting all the activity he'd done that day, but he wasn't going to let that stop him.

She shook her head. "Men. You and Jared are too much alike. I wouldn't be surprised if he tried climbing the house again with his cast on."

He crossed to the door and opened it. "I wouldn't be surprised, either."

"I was hoping you would disagree with me." Kathleen came out onto the porch. "Now every time the phone rings, I'll wonder what else he has gotten himself into."

"My little brother used to be the same way. I had to get him out of a lot of scrapes."

"Does he live here? New Orleans?"

This was the reason he didn't like to talk about himself. So often it led to questions he didn't want to answer. "I haven't seen him since he was four."

The front door swung open and Kip, with his eyes huge, thrust the phone into Kathleen's hands. "It's Nana. She says Hurricane Naomi has made an almost one-hundred-eighty-degree turn and picked up speed—lots of speed—and is heading straight for Hope. It should be here by tomorrow night."

Chapter Four

Kathleen clutched the phone with a trembling hand, hoping somehow Kip hadn't heard her mother right. "Mom, what's going on?"

"Exactly what Kip told you. The hurricane is coming right for us. It has picked up speed. This time I don't think we're going to dodge the bullet."

Kathleen's eyes closed, and she drew in a deep, fortifying breath. "He said tomorrow night—early or late?"

"It will start by early evening, and the eye should be going over us right after midnight if it continues to move at the same speed it is now."

"I guess you don't have to put up those supplies after all. We'll take care of this house and come over to help you after that."

Kathleen hung up and passed the phone to Kip. "You and your brother need to go to bed. First thing tomorrow, we'll have to board and tape up this house then help Nana."

Kip's eyes widened. "How bad will it be?"

Gideon stepped forward. "A lot of wind and rain."

"Like a bad thunderstorm?" Her son gripped the phone tighter.

Gideon settled his hand on Kip's shoulder. "Yeah. You'll be okay."

"Does this mean we don't have school tomorrow?"

"Yes. We'll be busy getting ready as will everyone else." Kathleen opened the screen door.

"Cool. Wait till Jared hears this."

"I don't want any more fighting between you and Jared. We have other things to deal with right now. Okay?"

Kip spun around and charged back into the house, saying, "Yes."

Turning to face Gideon, she let the screen door bang closed. "The last time I was in a hurricane was over twenty years ago. I've forgotten what to do. I remember Mom filling the bathtub and other containers with water. Getting candles, lanterns, batteries for a radio and flashlights..." With memories racing through her mind, it went blank.

"Stock up on food you don't have to refrigerate. We will most likely lose our electricity. Bring indoors everything that can be picked up by high winds. Since this house doesn't have hurricane shutters, tape or board the windows. Then pray. Are you going to stay here?"

"I don't know. I might go to Mom's."

"I think that would be better. If there is a big storm surge, this house could be flooded. It's nearer the beach than your mom's."

"Then that's where we'll be."

Gideon stared down at his cast. "If it wasn't for this, I'd be at the fire station." Frustration edged his voice.

"I'm on the B team at the hospital. I work post-hurricane. I'll contact work tomorrow morning and see when they want me to come in. There's so much to be done. This house isn't prepared."

He took her hand. "Get a good night's sleep, and I'll come over and help tomorrow morning first thing."

"Only if you'll let me help you."

"I have hurricane shutters, which will cut down on what I have to do. Let's get your house and your mom's prepared first. There shouldn't be too much to do with mine."

"I'll have breakfast ready at 6:30. At least let me feed you before you work."

He squeezed her hand then dropped it and turned toward the steps. "You've got yourself a date. See you at 6:30."

Kathleen stood on her porch and watched him

stroll down her sidewalk, hop into his Jeep and leave. As his taillights disappeared down the street, she peered up at the sky. Roiling clouds obscured the moon. It had begun.

The next morning, using the electric screw-driver that Gideon brought, Kathleen secured a large board over the picture window in the living room while Gideon held it in place for her. When she finished with the last screw, she descended the ladder and stepped back. "I hope that will hold."

"You've done what you can." He hoisted the ladder with his good arm and moved toward the detached garage behind the house.

Kathleen followed Gideon toward the backyard where Jared and Kip were hauling the patio items to the garage to store them. She passed several smaller windows she and Gideon had taped in the past hour since they had eaten breakfast.

"You haven't done your share of the work. I've been carrying all the heavy stuff," Kip yelled from the backyard.

Rounding the side of the house, Kathleen found Jared and Kip playing tug-of-war with a seat cushion. She slowed and shook her head. "I guess I should be thankful this hasn't happened before this. Kip still hasn't forgiven Jared for the homework last night."

"I seem to remember Zach and I fighting over nothing at times," Gideon said with a chuckle. "He used to love to bug me."

"I got this first. You take the table." Jared jerked the cushion toward him.

Kip let go of it. "Fine. Take it."

Jared staggered back and fell on his bottom into a puddle of water left by the rain during the night.

Stomping to the table, Kip lifted it and headed for the garage. When he saw Kathleen, his mouth pressed together in a thin line.

"Mom, did you see him?" Jared scampered to his feet and turned his back to her, showing her his jeans soaking wet with muddy water. "Look at this."

Kathleen inspected the dark clouds surging over them. "Jared, go in and change. Kip, you can help us finish clearing the patio."

"Jared doesn't have to work?" Kip disappeared into the garage.

"I'm counting to ten before I answer that one," Kathleen said to Gideon then trailed her son into the garage. She covered the space between them and blocked his path. "This is not a time for fighting. We have to get this house, Nana's and then Gideon's ready for the hurricane that will be here soon. If you two don't want to be grounded for the rest of your life, you'll work together and be civil with each other."

Tears welled into Kip's eyes. "I'm scared. I've listened to what they've said about hurricanes. I don't want to be here. Why did we move here?"

Kathleen knelt in front of her son and clasped his arms. "Honey, you'll be all right. We are preparing for it. This town has gone through hurricanes before, and it is fine. It has been here for almost two hundred years. It will be here for another two hundred."

"Don't be a scaredy-cat," Jared said from the doorway into the garage.

"Come here, Jared." Kathleen waved her hand toward him. When he approached warily, she took his hand. "We are a family, and we stick together, especially through trying times like this. I told Kip and now I'll tell you, Jared. We can't fight a hurricane and each other. I depend on you two for your help and cooperation."

Jared squared his shoulders and thrust out his chin. "I'll protect you. I'm not scared, Mom."

Kip yanked free from Kathleen and stormed toward the exit. "I'm not, either."

Jared opened his mouth to reply to his brother. Kathleen put two fingers over his lips. "Shh. Not a word. This may seem like an adventure to you, but it's a serious situation that could be dangerous. Like climbing up to the roof. Look what happened when you did that."

"It's starting to rain again." Gideon came into the garage, hauling part of a wooden lounge chair while Kip had the other end. "This is the last of the furniture. Let's get to your mom's and see what needs to be done there."

Kathleen rose. "That's a good idea. I want to get there before Nana decides to climb the ladder and close her hurricane shutters on the second floor."

"I can do that." Eagerness lit Jared's face.

Suddenly, Kathleen pictured her young son with a cast on each arm. "No more climbing for you for a while."

Kip stepped forward, his chest thrust out. "I'll do it."

"No. I'm going to." Kathleen headed into the house to get her purse. "You two go and get into the car."

Gideon followed her inside. "I'll meet you at your mom's."

She snatched her handbag from the kitchen counter and started out to the garage. Gideon touched her arm, the feel of his fingers momentarily grazing her skin, stopping her.

"Everything will be all right. We had a storm the first year I was here. A lot of wind and rain, but the town came through it."

"I hope so. I'm on the team that reports to the hospital right after the storm passes. I hate leaving my boys even then, but at least they'll be with Mom."

"I hate that I can't be out there helping, but my captain told me in no uncertain terms when I called him this morning not to come. Then he went on to give me his brief lecture on being injured. But it's hard standing on the sidelines watching others do what you feel you should."

"If you don't take care of yourself, you'll hurt yourself even more. Cracked ribs and a broken arm take time to heal."

He smiled. "I've never been a good patient."

"I'm used to that."

He strode toward the door. "We'd better go before it really starts raining. The few showers we've had are nothing compared to what will be coming soon."

"I'll follow you to Mom's."

In the car, Kathleen switched on the engine and backed out onto the street as Gideon climbed into his Jeep. Sprinkles fell onto the windshield. Silence ruled in the car. Glares were exchanged between her sons in the backseat. She clasped the steering wheel in such a tight grip, her knuckles whitened. The day had only begun. Before it ended, they would be drenched in water and hammered with wind.

* * *

"Mom, please get down from there. I can do that." Kathleen raced toward her mother, who was on the ladder against the house.

Ruth perched on one of the top rungs, wrestling with the wind to close the shutter. After finally shutting it, she swung around to stare down at her daughter. "What took y'all so long? I've got to go to the filling station and get gas. I only have a fourth of a tank. I should know better with a hurricane out in the Gulf. I always keep it topped off. But the storm fooled me when it turned toward Florida."

Ruth took a step down, lost her footing and began to fall. When she clutched the ladder, it teetered. Gideon hurried past Kathleen and grabbed it with one hand and steadied it against the house. Ruth sagged against the rungs.

Slowly she made her way down to the ground and collapsed back against the ladder, her hands shaking. "My word, I had visions of me landing in the same spot as Jared, but I can tell you I would not be able to bounce to my feet like he did. And a broken arm would be the least of my worries."

"Exactly, Mom. I told you I would do it."

"I'm gladly turning the job over to you—on one condition." Her mother swept around toward Gideon. "You need to hold the ladder for her. The rungs are a little slippery and the wind is picking up. I'll take the boys to the filling station with me."

"I've got a better idea. Take Jared. Kip will stay and help us." Kathleen picked up the ladder and moved it to the next window.

As the boys slowly walked across the front lawn, their heads down, their arms hanging listlessly at their sides, her mother leaned close to Kathleen and said, "Do you really want to do that? They will fight because one got to go with me."

"Yes. I have a project for Kip."

"Okay, I've warned you. I'll send him over here." She sauntered to the boys, spoke to them and then Jared cheered while Kip trudged toward Kathleen with his shoulders slumped even more.

"I need you to go next door and tell Miss Alice we'll be over to her house to help her just as soon as we get through here. Then stay and make sure everything outside is put in for her." Kathleen ascended the first rung.

"Aw, Mom, do I have to? She's mean. She yelled at Jared and me when we came into her yard to get a soccer ball last week."

Clinging to the ladder, Kathleen shifted around so she could peer down at Kip. "Yes, you have to. We help our neighbors, especially in times of need."

"But, Mom, she isn't our neighbor."

"Go. I've got to get these shutters closed." She waved her hand at Kip in the direction of Miss Alice's house.

When Kip stomped off, splashing water in the soggy grass as he went, Gideon used his lower limbs to anchor the ladder. "You are asking a lot of Kip."

"Tell you a secret. When I was a little girl, she scared me, too. But she is eighty-six and not getting around like she used to. She'll need help through this hurricane."

"I already have it taken care of. Pete is coming over to help me with a couple of the older residents' houses."

"Doesn't he have to work at the fire station?"

"Like the hospital they have two shifts. No one can do a good job if they are dead tired. He's on the second shift after the hurricane passes."

Kathleen proceeded up the ladder and fought to close the shutter, then she descended and started all over with the next one. Three windows later, Kip ran back across the yard.

"Mom. Mom!"

Kathleen jumped down several rungs to the ground and hastened toward her son. "What's wrong?"

"It's Old Lady Beggs. I knocked and knocked, but she didn't come to the door. I peeked through the window. She's sitting in a chair, her eyes closed, her head to the side." Kip stood in the middle of the yard, chewing on his fingernail. "I really banged loud on the door. She didn't move at all. I think she's dead."

"Honey, you stay here. I'll go check." Kathleen started across the lawn.

"I'm coming, too. Kip, when my friend, Pete, comes, tell him where we are."

"Can't I come?"

Both Kathleen and Gideon halted and whirled around. "No."

Kathleen glanced at Gideon and then continued her trek toward Miss Alice's house. On the woman's porch, Gideon pounded on the door while Kathleen checked through the open draperies into the living room. Just as Kip said, she lounged in a chair with her feet propped up and her head lolled to the side, one arm dangling toward the floor.

"Kip might be right. She isn't moving. We need to break in and get her some help."

Gideon came to Kathleen's side. "If she is alive, she isn't gonna like it."

"Do you think she has a spare key somewhere?"

Gideon looked under the welcome mat. When he rose, he shook his head. "This door is pretty sturdy. I don't think I can break it down without an ax, which I left at work. I'll go around and check the windows and back door. Maybe something is unlocked, and I can get in that way."

"Hurry. She might have lost consciousness. I'm calling 911 to be on the safe side."

Gideon started for the back, checking the windows as he went while Kathleen called 911 on her cell. The operator was dispatching an ambulance immediately.

Two minutes later, as Kathleen watched the old lady in the recliner for any signs of life, her white cat came charging into the living room from the kitchen, leaped and landed in the woman's lap. Miss Alice shot straight up at the same time Gideon barged into the room. Miss Alice let out a rip-roaring scream.

Gideon skidded to a stop, his eyes round, his face pale. He said something to Miss Alice, but Kathleen couldn't hear over the yelling. The woman wasn't even looking at Gideon. She stared right at Kathleen, who stood at her window peering inside.

Gideon moved toward her and bent down toward the woman. Miss Alice blinked, clutching her cat to her chest and glaring at Gideon as if he were a total stranger breaking into her house. He backed toward the front door and opened it.

"Kathleen, come in, please." The stress on the word *please* quickened her pace into the house.

As she passed the mirror in the hallway, Kathleen caught sight of herself and paused. From the occasional rain, her wet hair lay plastered against her head and her mascara ran down her face in a couple of places. And Gideon hadn't said a word to her. She scrubbed the black streaks from her cheeks and kept going into the living room.

"What did you say, young man?"

"We thought you were ill. We knocked on the door." His voice rose with each word he said.

Miss Alice shook her head and held up her hand. "Wait a minute." She fiddled with something in her ear then said, "My batteries must be going in my hearing aid. Help me up, young man."

Gideon did as instructed, and Miss Alice shuffled toward the kitchen, yelling, "I'll be right back."

When she left, Kathleen came to Gideon. "Why didn't you tell me I looked like a drenched raccoon?"

He looked away, a sheepish expression taking over his face. "I know better than to tell a woman that. I thought Kip would say something and get me off the hook."

"I scared the poor woman."

"I didn't think anything scared her. I thought she scared others. At least that's what the boys in my youth group have said when they found out I lived down the street from Alice Beggs." He put his finger into his ear and wiggled it. "I think my hearing is damaged. There is nothing wrong with her lungs."

"I heard that, young man." The woman appeared in the entrance to the dining room. "I should call the police. You broke into my house."

"Oh, no. I've got to call 911 back." Kathleen dug into her pocket for her cell.

Miss Alice's wrinkled forehead wrinkled even more. "You've already called 911 on him?"

Kathleen put the numbers into the phone. "No. For an ambulance. For you."

While she told the 911 operator that Alice Beggs was all right, the older lady shuffled her feet toward her recliner, shaking her head. "I was taking a nap. Can't a woman do that without everyone thinking she's dying? I need more beauty rest than when I was younger." She held out her hand toward Gideon. "Be useful. Help me into this chair, young man."

As Gideon took Miss Alice's arm to assist her into her recliner, Kathleen hung up. "We're sorry to disturb you, but my son thought something might be wrong with you. We knocked a long time on the door, but you didn't move."

"That's because I finally got to sleep after being up most of the night. Why in the world was your son over here trying to wake me up?"

"To see if you needed any help." Kathleen stuffed her cell back into her pocket.

"Yeah, help sleeping. No thanks to y'all."

Kathleen sighed, drawing on her patience she had stored up for dealing with her sons. "I thought we could get your house ready for the hurricane."

"What hurricane? Didn't you hear it's going to hit Florida?"

"No, Miss Alice, it's heading for Hope."

"Where's your mother? She told me yesterday morning we were safe, that it's going the other way."

"It changed its course."

"Why in the world can't it make up its mind? Reminds me of some women I know. No wonder men don't understand us. We don't understand ourselves." Miss Alice leaned back in the chair, fumbling at the side to lift the leg rest.

Gideon stooped and did it for her. "You're perfectly right."

Miss Alice swiveled her attention toward him. "You live down the street, don't you, young man?"

"Two houses away."

"Ah, yes. I've admired you when you've gone jogging."

Gideon's face reddened.

"Miss Alice, your windows need to be covered and—"

The older lady swung her gaze toward the picture window, jerked back and screamed.

Kathleen and Gideon pivoted to see Kip's face pressed against the pane.

Kathleen relaxed and waved him toward the front door. "Sorry, that's my son who was worried something was wrong with you." The one who didn't follow instructions to stay put.

She strode toward the front door to tell him to go back to Nana's, but the second she opened it, Miss Alice shouted, "Have him come in here."

Kip heard the words and shook his head, whispering, "No way, Mom. She's gonna yell at me."

Kathleen took Kip's hand. "I'll be with you."

He took baby steps toward the living room, hanging back from Kathleen. "My friends say she hates kids."

"What did you say, young'n?"

Kip's eyes widened, and he stopped dead in his tracks.

Miss Alice tried to turn her body to glimpse Kip, but she couldn't all the way. "C'mon in. I can't see you from there."

Kip moved forward a few more paces but dropped his head and stared at his feet as he dragged them across the floor.

"So you are Ruth's grandson. I've seen you a couple of times with another little boy. Who is he?"

"That's my other son, Jared."

Miss Alice ignored Kathleen and said to Kip, "What's the matter? Cat got your tongue?"

Kip kept his eyes on the floor.

"Can't you speak for yourself?" Miss Alice's lips thinned and almost disappeared completely. "Where are your manners? I'm here, not on the floor. Look at me when I talk to you."

Slowly Kip lifted his head, but his gaze focused on her chin, the lower part.

"That's better. I'm perfectly fine, but thank you for caring enough to go get help when you thought something was wrong." She flipped her hand toward the door. "Now you can git."

Kip didn't wait for another word. He whirled and ran out the front door and off the porch.

Miss Alice chuckled. "He's braver than most. But that's no surprise since he's Ruth's grandson. Where is your mother?"

"Getting gas because of the hurricane."

Gideon glanced outside, then back at the woman. "Miss Alice, can we board up your windows for you?"

"Don't have any boards. Haven't had a hurricane in years that amounted to much. Not like back in sixty-nine."

"Then we can tape most of them, and I can see if I can get a piece of plywood for your picture window." Gideon turned to Kathleen. "Unless your mom has a tape measure, I'll need to get mine."

Miss Alice twisted her mouth into a thoughtful look. "Who's going to remove all that after the hurricane? I certainly can't."

"I will," Gideon answered before Kathleen could reply. "We'd better leave and get your mom's house done, so we can come over here."

"When is this hurricane coming?" Miss Alice pushed the lever down so her footrest dropped, then she scooted to the chair's edge. "I haven't got all my supplies. I'm not prepared at all."

"Kip knows where the tape measure is. Go have him get it for you," Kathleen said to Gideon, then she put her hand under Miss Alice's arm. "Let's go look at what you have. We'll make a list of what you need, and I'll go get it for you."

"Bless you, child. Hurricane Naomi kept dancing around out in the Gulf, playing with us, that I just forgot about her after a while. Same thing happened a couple of years ago and nothing occurred. Thought that was what would happen this time. Don't keep up with things like I used to."

As Gideon left, Kathleen escorted her mom's neighbor toward the kitchen. The thought of the shutters on the second floor windows in the back of her mother's house still needing to be closed lent a certain urgency to her steps until she realized Miss Alice only moved in slow motion. Contrary to what she'd heard, Hurricane Naomi was finally doing in the Gulf.

Chapter Five

"This will teach me to keep my gas tank filled when there's a hurricane out in the Gulf." Kathleen's mother stood up after scrubbing the bathtub out and making sure the stopper was secured before turning on the water. "There, that is the last one. Both tubs will have water in them."

Kathleen took the cleaning supplies and put them back under the bathroom sink. "I wasn't able to fill Miss Alice's order totally, but I think she'll have enough batteries for her flashlights and radio."

"At least you didn't sit in line at the gas station for three hours only to be told I get five gallons and that is it. Of course, it seemed like half the people in Hope were in that line."

"I didn't have to stand in line because there was little left on the shelves at the store. The other half of the town must have struck the grocery stores."

"Nope. They're on the road evacuating. Are you sure you don't want to take the boys and go to Aunt Cora's?"

"I can't. I have to go to the hospital right after it passes. You could take the boys."

"No, she only lives about fifty miles north of here. This house sits up on a hill and has never gotten any water. The wind wouldn't be much less than here. But I can go if you want. I'll probably have enough gas to get to my sister's."

"If you don't get caught up in traffic. I can't take the chance of you running out of gas, and I wouldn't trust my car on the road the way it's acting up." All morning Kathleen had wrestled with whether to send her children away with her mother to Aunt Cora's. Jared had flat out told her that he wanted to stay and see the hurricane while Kip told her he wouldn't leave her.

Her mother left the bathroom. "You need to take my car to the hospital when you have to report to work after the hurricane. I'm certainly not going to be going anywhere."

Kathleen headed back to the kitchen where the boys were helping Gideon fill jugs and other containers with water. "Mom, will you ask Miss Alice to come here to stay this evening? I hate her being by herself, but she wouldn't come when Gideon and I tried to get her to."

"I'll try. But she is a stubborn old lady."

Kathleen clamped her teeth down to keep from replying, "Kinda like you." She went into the kitchen to find the water containers all over the counter.

While her mother shrugged into her rain gear and rubber boots, Kip and Jared faced Kathleen with big grins. "We did this," Kip said, gesturing toward the jugs. "Gideon supervised. We did the work. Three gallons of water for each person a day. Isn't that right, Gideon?"

"You've got it. I think y'all are set."

"Did you get yours done when you went home a while ago?"

"Yep. My house is battened down and as secure as it can be. I have my supplies and enough water for a couple of weeks."

Kathleen scanned the kitchen. "The same here."

"Are we staying at Nana's tonight?" Kip started carrying the jugs of water to the pantry on an inside wall.

"We don't want Nana to be alone," Jared added while lugging his share across the room.

"Yeah, we're staying." Kathleen helped her sons store the containers.

"How about Miss Alice?" Kip asked when he came out of the walk-in pantry.

"I'm going right now to see if I can convince her to come over here." Her mother put on her rain hat and tied it down.

"Can I go, too?" Kip crossed the kitchen to his grandmother.

"It's okay with me if your mom says okay."

Kip spun around and asked her, "Can I?"

"Fine. Wear you raincoat and stay with Nana. It's starting to get windy out there."

Jared came out of the food closet. "You're gonna go see Old Lady Beggs? She yells."

"I didn't say anything the first time I heard that name, but I don't want to hear you two call her that. Either use Miss Alice or Miss Beggs. Understand, Kip?" Kathleen peered at him, then turned to her younger son. "Jared?"

They nodded.

As Kip left with her mother, Jared took another jug to the pantry. "I've got to make sure Bubbles has enough water. Can I go check and fill the bowl up?"

"Sure."

When Jared left, Gideon asked, "Bubbles? I didn't know you had a pet."

"A goldfish. The boys want a dog for Christmas along with a whole list of other things, the top of the list being bikes that are not girl ones like Mom has."

"Christmas? That's two months away."

"Yeah, I know, but they are already thinking about it. Their idea of Christmas is so commercial, and no matter how much I tell them this year that we'll celebrate on a smaller scale, they don't listen."

The door flew open, bringing in rain and wind as Kathleen's mother and Kip entered. "Whew. It's starting to get nasty out there," she said as she untied her rain hat and hung everything on a peg in the mudroom off the kitchen. "We ran back. I've had my exercise for the month today."

"Where's Miss Alice?" Kathleen leaned back against the counter next to Gideon.

"She doesn't like crowds. Told Nana she would be just fine at her house. She planned on turning off her hearing aid and sleeping through the whole thing."

Her mother emerged from the mudroom, fingering her damp hair. "Actually, I don't blame her. It's getting wet out there, and she moves so slowly."

Gideon released a long breath. "I'd better head home then. Butch doesn't like loud noises."

Kip giggled. "Butch is a funny name for a girly dog."

"Hey, he'll take offense if he hears you say that."

"Yeah, and he might nip my ankle if he did." Kip covered his mouth to keep his laughter inside.

"Why don't you bring Butch and come ride out the hurricane here with us? I personally don't like being alone in a storm." Her mother averted her head, suddenly sliding her gaze away from Gideon.

But Kathleen didn't need to see her expression to know what her mom was up to. Gideon was an available bachelor, and her daughter was available now. Bingo. Why not get them together? As that went through her mind, Kathleen said without really thinking about it, "I agree. You shouldn't be alone. You're injured. I wouldn't want you to do anything to strain your cracked ribs."

"Right, Kathleen has a point."

"Yeah, Gideon, please stay and bring Butch." Kip took his hand and dragged him toward the mudroom where the rain gear was. "I'll come with you and carry your dog."

"I think I'm being bulldozed by all of you."

"If that means we're ganging up on you, yep, we are. I don't want to be the man of the house. I've never been in a hurricane."

Hearing Kip say that twisted Kathleen's heart. Ever since his dad had died last year, he'd tried to be the man of the house because some of their friends in Denver had said that the job was his now that his father was gone. Although he'd only been eight, he'd taken the role seriously to the point of even bossing Jared around right after Derek's death. That was what had started the fighting between them that had escalated when they'd moved to Hope.

Gideon captured Kathleen's gaze and held it for a long moment. For a brief time a connection between her and Gideon sprang up, taking her by surprise in its strength. They had spent the whole day helping each other and neighbors get ready for the hurricane. Even with his broken arm, he'd managed to participate fully in the preparations and get her sons involved, without any arguing.

"Is it okay if Kip helps me bring Butch?"

Kathleen's throat swelled at the emotions sweeping through her—seeing the eagerness on Kip's face, the compassion on Gideon's as if he knew how much her sons needed a man's influence. "Yes, but hurry."

The clash of thunder boomed as Gideon unlocked his front door. The forty-mile-per-hour wind whipped his poncho about him. Kip huddled close, letting the house block some of it. The second the boy could he charged into the foyer, dripping water all over the tiles.

He glanced down at the puddle forming on the floor. "Sorry."

"If that is all this place gets, I'll be happy. Butch!" Gideon headed toward the back.

His bichon frise yelped, the sound coming from the den. When he entered, he saw the white curly tail sticking out from under the couch. "Butch, come on. We're leaving."

The dog whined, trying to burrow deeper under the sofa.

"What's wrong?" Kip moved toward Butch.

"He's scared. Loud thunderstorms really bother him."

Kip stooped and bent down to look under the couch. "It's okay, Butch. I'm scared, too. We can take care of each other. I won't let anything happen to you."

His coaxing voice held a soothing quality that Gideon's dog responded to. He shifted until his face pressed against Kip's leg. The boy stroked him, continuing to murmur reassurances.

"I'm going to grab a couple of things. I'll be right back." Gideon left the two to bond and went down his hallway to his bedroom.

He retrieved a duffel bag out of the closet and stuck in a high-powered flashlight and then went to the garage for some tools he might need right after the storm. As he gathered his supplies, he thought back to that moment in the kitchen when he and Kathleen had looked at each other. For a moment he saw a future with her. Until he remembered that anyone he had really loved had been taken from him. Usually he could suppress the pain of a loss, but locking gazes with her made him remember the last time he'd seen his baby brother or his parents right before the fire that had taken their lives. His shoulders slumped and his head dropped as the memories washed over him.

"Gideon, Butch is ready to leave," Kip said from the kitchen door to the garage. "I told him I would hold him tight and not let the wind get him."

Gideon sucked in a deep breath, zipped up his duffel bag and rotated toward the boy, forcing a look of reassurance on his face. "First, I need to disconnect some appliances since there's a good chance the electricity will go off."

"That happened in Denver to us during a snowstorm. It got cold in the house. We didn't have electricity for a day." Kip cradled Butch against his chest.

"It might be off longer than that here." Gideon made his way through his house and unplugged various items like his computer and television set. When he was finished, he strode toward the foyer. "Let's get back to your grandma's."

"How long?" Kip stepped out onto the porch, shielding Butch from the wind.

"Could be a week. Could be shorter than that, but it could be longer."

"Longer?" Kip shouted over the howl of the wind and another clap of thunder.

"That's why we have supplies for a couple of

weeks. To be prepared." Gideon hurried his pace, crossing Miss Alice's yard and glancing toward her boarded front window. Light leaked out of the slits around the edges of the two-by-fours he found to cover it.

When they reached Ruth's porch, Gideon glanced down at Kip. He chewed his bottom lip and clutched Butch tight against him. Gideon put his bag down and clasped the boy's shoulder. He lifted his gaze to Gideon's.

"It's always wise to prepare for the worst, but that doesn't mean it will happen. Worrying won't change what is to be. We'll deal with whatever happens. The Lord is with us."

"Mom used to say that. She doesn't anymore."

The front door swung open, and Kathleen stood in the entrance. "I was beginning to worry about you two."

Kip entered, saying, "I had to coax Butch out from under the couch. He's scared." He kept going down the hall to the den.

Gideon moved into the house. "Sorry. I also decided to turn off some of my major appliances in case there were electrical surges."

"Is everything all right? Kip was frowning."

"He's concerned about the electricity going out for a long time."

"Then I'd better not tell him I am, too. I try to reassure him as much as possible, but he worries about everything. It has gotten worse since Derek died. Whereas Jared is fearless, Kip is the opposite."

"I went through that as a boy when my parents died. I cried all the time. I didn't understand why they weren't coming back for Zach and me."

"When anything changes, he freaks out."

"I did, too. That's probably why I didn't do well in a lot of my foster care homes. Things changed all the time. When I couldn't control my life, I acted out. It took me growing up and getting to know the Lord to change that reaction. I'm trying to let Him control my life. But it isn't always easy to do."

"I used to feel that way and look what happened. My husband died and left me with a ton of debt to pay off. To top that, my boys are hurting with everything that has happened. To make ends meet, I had to move here, and they weren't happy about that."

"Because it is a change. Kids depend on stability."

"I wouldn't mind it, either."

He stepped closer in the foyer. "Whether we want it or not, chaos is coming in the form of Hurricane Naomi."

Jared came out of the den. "Kip won't let me hold Butch. I should get a turn, too."

"Ah, I wondered when Kip and Jared's truce

would end," she whispered to Gideon then walked toward her son.

He'd wanted to ask questions about her situation, but this wasn't the time. There might never be a good time. It wasn't his business, but he cared about her and beneath her words he heard the pain she carried.

Wind and rain slashed at Kathleen's childhood home as though beating its fists against the exterior and demanding entrance. Sitting in a chair that Gideon had brought into the laundry room—the only interior room in the house—she watched her sons play Go Fish in the glow of the flashlight. Seated in the corner, her mother listened to the radio for any news concerning the hurricane raging outside. The howl of the wind continually pulled Kip's attention away from the game, to the frustration of his little brother.

"Why do we have to stay in here? I can't see what's going on." Jared tossed down his cards after losing again to his brother. "I'm bored."

Kathleen gestured toward two pallets on the floor. "Then try and sleep."

Jared shot her a look as if she'd gone crazy. "What if something happens? I've got to be ready."

Butch yelped at the door right before it opened,

and Gideon came into the room. "Everything looks okay right now."

Static suddenly filled the air. "Oh, great, the radio station has been knocked off the air," her mother muttered.

His eyes huge, Kip scooped up Butch. "Did the hurricane get it?"

Her mother turned off the static noise. "No, honey. They either lost their backup power or the storm is interfering with their signal. Nothing to be concerned about."

Gideon picked his way through the pillows and blankets littering the floor to Kathleen and sat next to her. "The electricity is off up and down the street. I don't see any evidence of flooding." He turned his head away from the boys and lowered his voice, "But I think one of us should go out and check every fifteen minutes. The wind has picked up, and I see debris everywhere."

"I'll go next."

"Go where, Mom?" Kip asked, holding the dog close to him, laying his cheek against the animal.

"Just to check the house. We don't have windows in here to look out so it's a good thing to do that every once in a while."

"Why don't we camp out in the den? It's more comfortable." Standing against the washing machine, Kip followed Bubbles swimming around in circles.

"It's safer staying away from windows," Kathleen's mother answered, turning the radio on again and finding more static. Frowning, she switched it off.

The steady sound of the rain and wind hung in the silence that had descended. Even Jared bit his lower lip and hunkered down on the pallet.

"Why don't you listen to your music on your MP3 player?" Kathleen wished she had one to take her mind off the hurricane.

"I forgot mine at home when we packed our bags." Kip flinched when the noise increased in intensity.

"I've got mine." Jared reached for his backpack and dug into it. When he found it, he stuck the earplugs in and lay on the pallet.

The relentless sound pounding at the house continued. Kip chewed on his fingernails, looking at the ceiling. Finally he curled up on his blankets, burying Butch and him beneath the covers.

"I hope he goes to sleep, but I don't think that's going to happen," Kathleen whispered to Gideon.

The blanket flipped back and Kip sat up. "I heard you. I can't sleep. Who can with all this noise?"

"Then why don't you tell me about the snowstorm you had in Denver where you lost your power. How many inches was it?" Gideon leaned forward, clasping his hands, resting his elbows on his thighs.

A crack and boom rent the air. Kip shot to his feet. Butch burrowed deeper into the covers. "What was that?"

"Tell Gideon about the snowstorm. I'll go check." Kathleen schooled her voice and her expression into a calmness she didn't feel. Inside, her heart thundered against her chest, and she squeezed her hands into fists to keep them from trembling. Kip didn't need to see that.

She pushed to her feet and hurried out of the room before her son saw fear on her face. Another sound reverberated through the air. Like a tree crashing into something nearby.

Since most of the windows were shuttered, Kathleen went to the front door and opened it slowly. It was protected from the direction the wind was coming, but she didn't want to take any chances. She knew the folly of going out in the storm, but she needed to discover the source of that noise. The yard had tall pines and live oak in it. She moved a couple of feet out onto the porch with Gideon's powerful flashlight.

When she peered out at the rain and wind lashing the ground at a forty-five-degree angle, she couldn't see anything. Through the early morning light she accounted for all the trees in front. As she started to back away and close the door, she noticed out of the corner of her eye the base of an uprooted pine in Miss Alice's yard.

Quickly going into the house, Kathleen slammed the door closed and rushed into the garage where there was a taped window that faced Miss Alice's place. Through the strips she spied the pine. Its massive trunk halved the one-story house right where Miss Alice's bedroom was. Rain and wind whipped through the hole in the structure. Kathleen remembered the older woman had planned to sleep while Hurricane Naomi raged outside.

Chapter Six

❧

That Miss Alice was probably trapped beneath the pine tree gripped Kathleen with immobility for a few seconds as the howling wind vied with the drenching downpour. Then another crack followed by a boom propelled her into action. She whirled around and raced toward the door into the house. When she burst into the laundry room, Jared lay curled on his pallet, asleep finally, while Kip, buried by mounds of covers, stayed hidden with Butch.

Her mother glanced up. "What's wrong?"

In midstretch, Gideon riveted his attention to her.

"Miss Alice's house was struck by a tree right through her bedroom where she was going to be. We've got to help her."

Gideon bolted to his feet. "I'll go."

"No, not alone." Kathleen blocked his exit.

"Mom, remain here with the boys. If you can get through to 911, let them know about Miss Alice."

"Hon, I doubt I'll be able to, but I'll try. What if Jared or Kip wakes up?"

"Tell them we went to help Miss Alice, and we'll be right back." Kathleen spun on her heel and moved into the hallway, waiting until Gideon left and closed the door.

"I heard another tree either go down or split, but I didn't see where."

"You should stay here." Gideon began donning his rain gear.

When Kathleen finished snapping her water-proof jacket, she grabbed her heavy-duty flashlight and started for the back door. "I'm a nurse. If something is wrong with Miss Alice, I might be able to help."

Right behind her, he stopped her progress. "I'm a paramedic. Let me handle this. You take care of your family."

She tapped his cast underneath the rain slicker. "With only one arm?"

He scowled. "Let's go. Take hold of me and stay close."

As she stepped out into the wind, its force nearly snatched her flashlight from her. She tightened her grip and lowered her head. She dragged one foot forward, then another, fighting the cross-winds and the driving rain. The beating of her heart battered at her chest as the hurricane battered Hope.

Gideon paused near the downed tree, inspecting what he could, but the downpour and high winds made it hard to see anything. Hugging the side of Alice's house, Kathleen used it to shelter herself from the fierce storm and continued toward the back door. She reached it and tried the handle. Locked. She peered back toward Gideon approaching her.

"It's locked. How do we get in?" Kathleen asked.

"I'll try to climb in through the hole the tree has created. There's a gap. I might fit," he yelled over the din of the hurricane.

"I might be able to better than you. Let me try first."

"But—"

"I have two arms I can use to climb." She started back the way she'd come.

Gideon dogged her steps, and when she arrived at the place where he thought he could get into the house, Kathleen examined it and wondered how she would get through the slit. She grabbed hold of the trunk, the rain pummeling her. Gideon positioned himself next to the tree, and she used him to hike herself up and into the small opening.

The wet bark scraped against her as she wiggled through the hole. Her raincoat snagged on a broken branch, stopping her progress. She yanked on her slicker and freed it, then slithered through the rest of the opening.

With her flashlight she inspected the area where the tree came down. All she could see was the edge of the bed. The pine obscured the rest of it. She stepped closer and peered through the limbs to see if she saw Miss Alice. The storm still hammered at her.

She knelt next to the bed and probed the green foliage for any sign of Miss Alice. She couldn't see anything. "Miss Alice!" she yelled several times over the noise of the storm. Even though her neighbor had intended to turn off her hearing aid, she had to try in case Miss Alice hadn't.

Standing, she hurried into the hallway and closed the bedroom door to keep some of the wind and rain out although part of the corridor's ceiling had caved in as well. She headed toward the kitchen to open the door for Gideon.

After letting him into the house, she pointed toward the dining room and living room. "Let's check the house. I didn't see her in her bedroom. Maybe she used her other one. Or maybe she's on the other side of her bed where I can't get." As she voiced that last fear, she sent a silent prayer to the Lord that Miss Alice would be safe somewhere else in her house.

"We'll find her."

Kathleen swept her flashlight in a wide arc on

half the dining room while Gideon took the other part, making her way toward the living room. *Please let Miss Alice be safe in her recliner as before.*

But when Kathleen entered the room ahead of Gideon and shone her light on the chair, its emptiness mocked her. "Where's Miss Alice's cat? I haven't seen or heard it."

"With her probably. Or hiding."

A slamming sound caused Kathleen to jump, nearly falling back into Gideon. He steadied her with one hand, then skirted her and strode toward the noise. In the hallway he slowed his quick pace. Kathleen spied the bedroom door she'd shut banging against the wall as the wind whipped through.

"Let's finish checking the rest of the house then recheck her bedroom." Gideon covered the distance to Miss Alice's other bedroom.

Kathleen took the closed door across the hall. When she entered the bathroom, she came to a halt, her light illuminating a sleeping Miss Alice on a small, blow-up mattress with her cat curled next to her.

"Gideon, she's in here." Kathleen knelt next to Miss Alice and shook her shoulder.

The woman's eyes popped open. For a few seconds confusion marked her expression until recognition dawned in her gaze. "Why are you here?

I'm perfectly fine. I told you I was going to bed and sleep through this."

"Miss Alice, a pine tree fell on your house. On your bedroom. I was afraid you went to sleep in your bed."

The older woman's eyes grew round. "My bedroom? Something told me to set up in here. This is the only room without windows." She struggled to sit up.

Kathleen helped her. "Please come over to Mom's house. We'll help you. You've got a couple of other trees close to your house."

"I'll be all—"

Gideon moved into the bathroom. "Miss Alice, do you want us to worry about you? Because we will if you don't come with us. There is no way we can leave you here with your house damaged like it is."

"A tree could fall on Ruth's house."

Gideon plowed his hand through his wet hair. "Yep, you're certainly right, but right now one hasn't. At least wind and rain aren't blowing through her place."

"What about my things?"

"You're more important than any of your possessions. I'll help you carry what you think is important."

"I've got to take Cottonballs. I can't leave him here." Miss Alice scooped up her white cat and held it against her chest. "Help me up. My knees don't work like they used to."

Gideon took Miss Alice's left arm while Kathleen clasped her right one, and they hoisted her to her feet.

"I have to have my pocketbook. I don't go anywhere without it."

"Where is it?" Kathleen scooted the air mattress back so Miss Alice could walk unhindered.

"In the bathtub along with some of my most prized possessions. I need them, too."

"I'll get them while Gideon helps you."

"Miss Alice, you'll need to stay close to me. The wind is fierce."

"Don't you worry about me, young man. I've been through some bad storms before. You don't live to be eighty-six and not. I could tell you some stories…" As she and Gideon made their way toward the kitchen, the roar of the wind streaming from the bedroom drowned out her words.

Kathleen turned toward the bathtub and saw Miss Alice's purse along with a sack of other items. Taking the paper bag, she panned the room for something to put her possessions into that wouldn't fall apart the minute she stepped outside. Finally, she dumped the contents of the trash can out on the floor and stuffed the sack down into it, then hurried into the hall.

Her slicker flapped in the wind coming from

the bedroom. She didn't want to think of the damage being done to the inside of the house. In the kitchen, before she followed Gideon and Miss Alice and her cat out into the tempest, she drew in a fortifying breath.

Lord, please help us get back to Mom's safely.

A couple of hours later, Gideon opened the front door and stood in the entrance to Ruth's house, surveying the street. The rain still fell, backing up at the drains and flooding the road. He ran his fingers through his now-dry hair then kneaded the tight cords of his neck. Tension gripped him.

Limbs, leaves and debris cluttered the rain-soaked ground. Downed trees crisscrossed his neighbors' yards. A small magnolia in front of Ruth's lay uprooted and blocking the sidewalk. Months of work stretched before the town. It took a day to destroy, but it would take a long time to repair.

"How bad is it?" Kathleen came to his side to peer outside.

"We probably fared better than some areas nearer the water. The storm surge was supposed to be bad. I think most of those people evacuated. At least I hope they did."

She clicked off her flashlight. Although it was daylight, a steady rain grayed the sky, and the shuttered windows darkened the interior of the house. "I'm afraid of what I'll find at the cottage. It sits at a lower elevation near the beach."

"When do you have to report to work?"

"I should go in as soon as possible. The people who've been at the hospital have been there for over twenty-four hours."

"I want to drive you. You said your car has been giving you problems. I don't want you to get stranded."

"Thankfully, the hospital isn't but a few miles from here. If I have to, I can walk."

He turned toward her, grasping her arm. "No, I will take you. It's going to be dangerous with flooding and downed power lines."

"I hate leaving Mom and the boys, but they need me at the hospital."

"Don't worry about them. I can stay here and help."

"Don't let Miss Alice go home. It isn't safe."

He grinned. "I'll do my best, but she's stubborn. I thought for a moment last night I was going to have to throw her over my shoulder and carry her out of her house."

"That would have been a sight, especially with your cracked ribs and broken arm."

"Yeah, I was doing some heavy-duty praying she'd agree without a fight."

The look in Kathleen's eyes softened. She took

hold of his hand. "Thank you for being here. I think your presence helped the boys, especially Kip."

"It's much better to ride out a hurricane with someone than by yourself." Most of his life he had been by himself, but when he said that to Kathleen, he realized he meant every word. He'd felt needed and liked that feeling.

"I'd better get ready," Kathleen said with a deep sigh.

"I'll get my Jeep and be back to take you."

She turned back into the house and crossed to the hallway, using her flashlight to guide her. Gideon shut the front door and went to the kitchen to get into his rain gear, then he headed out the back and cut across Ruth's yard toward Miss Alice's, circling around toward the front. As he strode past her place, he took note of the extensive damage. Another tree had fallen on her porch and crashed through its roof, barely missing the main house.

When he arrived at his home, one of his shutters was ripped off its hinges and the window was broken, allowing rain into his place. He went inside and hurried to the front spare bedroom. Now that the wind wasn't driving the rain at an angle, water was no longer pooling on his hardwood floor. He would take Kathleen then come back to patch the hole the best he could. Maybe he could get Kathleen's sons to help him now that the rain had lessened and the wind had calmed. It would be good to keep them busy, especially Jared.

Ten minutes later he pulled up in front of Ruth's. Kathleen came out before he could get out of his Jeep. She hurried toward his car and climbed into the passenger's side.

"Jared wanted to come with us. I told him he can't leave the house until it's safe."

"I thought I would see if Kip and Jared would help me repair one of my windows. Other than some rain damage in that bedroom, I think my house weathered the storm okay. I noticed some shingles off the roof and some branches down but nothing like Miss Alice's place."

"I went upstairs and the ceiling in my old bedroom is leaking so I'm sure Mom's roof has some problems, too."

"There's a lot of work to do, but first I need to get you to the hospital."

He came to a stop at the end of the block where a downed tree impeded his progress. Climbing from the Jeep, he started for the medium-size pine to move it. He grasped it and started dragging it, a grimace of pain on his face. Kathleen joined him and took hold of it as he did. Together they managed to drag it off the road enough to allow cars around it.

Back in the Jeep a few minutes later Gideon threw the car into Drive and pulled forward. "That probably won't be the only time we'll be doing that." He steered clear of a power line down on one side of the street and continued toward the hospital.

By the time he reached the front doors of Hope Memorial, his hand ached from gripping the steering wheel so tightly and the tension in his neck had intensified. What little he'd seen of the town left an impression of chaos, as though he'd driven through a war-torn area.

When he parked, he angled toward Kathleen. "When do you want me to pick you up?"

"My shift will end tomorrow morning at this time. We'll rotate teams until things calm down, but from the looks of the town that may be a while."

"This is the worst possible time to be on medical leave."

"But you are for a good reason." She touched his cast.

He captured her hand and laced his fingers through hers. "I know, but it doesn't make it any easier to accept it. Thanks for trying to make me feel better. The department can't curtail my activities around the neighborhood, though. I can focus my energy helping people on my street. There will be a lot to do there."

Smiling, Kathleen shook her head. "Why does that not surprise me? Just remember it has been less than a week since you were injured. Don't overdo it and make your situation worse. Promise me you'll take breaks, at least."

The concern in her expression warmed him. She had a kind heart. From what he'd seen, that made her a good nurse. But she was able to do her job while he wasn't. He had never been an inactive person, and it would be hard to start now, especially with all that had to be done.

He cocked his mouth into a grin. "I promise. I want to get better so I can go back to work."

She leaned across the seat and gave him a quick kiss on the cheek then opened the door and slipped out of his Jeep, leaving him to wonder about that brief touch of her lips on his cheek. He closed his eyes for a few seconds and could imagine the kiss all over again. He could smell her lingering scent of vanilla. The sensations she'd produced in him had nothing to do with friendship. Whoa! This was not good. He had no business being anything other than a friend to Kathleen. Neither of them was looking for anything more.

"Mr. Miller in room 320 is finally settled down. Per the doctor's orders, I increased his pain meds." Kathleen took the chart of the older man who had broken a hip when he fell off a ladder. She made some notes, then placed it back behind the counter at the nurses' station.

"We've been so busy I never got to ask you how Ruth fared in the hurricane." Mildred eased into a chair and massaged her temples. "I don't think I've slept in forty-eight hours."

"Who can sleep through a hurricane?" Kathleen snapped her fingers. "Oh, I forgot. Miss Alice slept through a good part of it until Gideon and I came to rescue her. Then she was up with us in the laundry room, refereeing between her cat and Gideon's dog. Not a pretty sight. The cat kept hissing the whole time. A couple of times his banshee cry rivaled the noise of the storm."

"Ah, poor thing. Alice Beggs can be a handful."

"Mom!"

Kathleen peered toward the stairs and spied Jared and Kip racing toward her. She held up her hand to slow them down, but Jared crashed into a doctor coming out of a patient's room, knocking the distinguished-looking man to the floor while Kip skidded to a halt a foot from him. Not far behind the boys, Gideon came down the hall, a frown on his face.

"Sorry, Kathleen. They got ahead of me racing up the stairs."

The six-foot-five doctor picked himself up from

the floor and glared down at her sons. "No running in the hospital. We have injured people here, and I don't want to be one of them."

Jared leaned back and looked up at the man. "Sorry."

"What are you doing here?" Dr. Allen set his hands on his hips. "This isn't a playground."

"Mom works here." Jared pointed toward her, then turned his big eyes on the man, pure innocence in his expression. "I'm really sorry, sir. I won't run again."

And her son believed that until the next time. Kathleen quickly covered the space between Jared and Dr. Allen.

Dr. Allen straightened his white coat, saying, "I'm glad to hear that," then nodded toward her and made his way to another patient's room.

Jared grinned from ear to ear, turning on that little-boy look intended to melt her heart. "I'm sorry, Mom. I was just glad to see you."

"They worked so hard yesterday helping the neighbors and your mom clean up that I couldn't say no to coming with me to pick you up."

Jared spotted the head nurse behind the counter, waved and said in a loud voice that could carry beyond down the hall, "Hi, Miss Mildred. Do you need any help? I've been helping anyone that does."

Kip punched him in the arm. "Shh. This is a hospital. People are sleeping."

"But it's ten in the morning."

"Boys, why don't you go downstairs with Gideon? I'll be right there."

"We're parked in the left lot when you come out the front entrance. The other one is still blocked with a downed oak." Gideon grabbed Jared's hand before he shot for the stairs.

Mildred came up behind Kathleen. "Go home and sleep. Be with your sons. I'll see you in two days."

"Call me on my cell if someone can't come in. I don't live too far away, and we are in okay shape." With cell reception working some of the time, she'd talked to her mother yesterday evening, and she reconfirmed what Kathleen had thought. Her childhood home didn't have too much damage, especially compared to Miss Alice's house and others she saw on the way to the hospital.

"Knowing Ruth, she has the neighborhood organized with the cleanup."

Kathleen walked into the room behind the counter and pulled her purse out of her locker. "You know my mother well," she said with a laugh. "The trick will be getting some rest before I'm put on a work crew. How about you? When are you going home?"

"I'm camping out here for a few more days. I

don't have family and unfortunately my duplex near the beach didn't make it. Thankfully I was here, but one of my neighbors let me know when he went back after evacuating."

"Then you need to come to Mom's. She has the room."

"Aren't you and your sons staying with her? And how about Alice?"

"I hadn't planned on it, but with all that has happened here I haven't had time to check about Mom's rental I was living in. It wasn't as close as you were to the beach so it might be all right. Still, you know Mom will insist. You are like family."

Mildred smiled, a tired gesture because she'd been working for two straight days. "I'll think about it. Now you'd better go before your boys overpower that nice young man and come looking for you."

Kathleen laughed at the image that came to mind. "Don't forget there's a place for you if it doesn't work out at your sister's. The hospital isn't where you should stay. You'll work all the time."

"We're mighty busy, but I could use a break."

Kathleen hugged Mildred then walked toward the stairs. Five minutes later she climbed into the front passenger seat of Gideon's Jeep while Jared and Kip were sitting still and quiet.

"Okay, what have you done with my sons?" She slid a look toward the backseat.

"We're being good." Jared folded his hands in his lap.

"Yeah, Mom. We want to go to our house, and if we don't act good, Gideon will take us back to Nana's."

"Oh, I see." She straightened forward, slanting a glance toward Gideon. "We're going by the cottage?"

"Your mom wanted me to check on it. We've heard that area was flooded."

"Why didn't someone tell me?" She'd thought about it while working then another emergency had come in and she hadn't had time. That had been her past twenty-four hours—one crisis after another.

"Because your mom didn't want you to worry. We had so much to do in the neighborhood yesterday just to make it safe. We didn't have time for anything else. A couple of people have generators. One is keeping food cold. Another is where people can do their laundry. I brought mine down to your mom's since y'all and Miss Alice are staying there. Between those two generators they're cooking a hot meal for everyone on the street. Your mom has set up headquarters for the hurricane cleanup."

"Headquarters?"

"She has organized all of us. She's very good at getting things done."

"Miss Alice didn't demand to go home?"

"At first, until she saw her house. She may be stubborn, but she's not a fool. She's actually settled in at your mom's quite well. Now, her cat is another thing."

"Is Butch still there?"

He turned onto the street where the rental cottage was. "I fixed my window so there won't be anymore rain damage, and Butch is happily back at his house."

Kathleen scanned the houses where she lived, sucking in a deep breath and holding it. The sight of the destruction churned her stomach. She could see where the water had come up to houses—some over their first story. The smell of rotting vegetation and rancid water saturated the air, causing her stomach to roil even more.

Gideon pulled into the driveway and switched off his engine. The silence from the backseat spoke of the horrific sight where the cottage used to be. All that was left was the foundation with pieces of what could be their place scattered around it, but Kathleen couldn't tell for sure. The neighboring homes were gone too, as if a surge of water had focused its power on this area that dipped down. It probably had formed a river in the middle of the hurricane.

"Mom, where are our things?" Kip finally asked in a choked voice.

"I don't know, honey. Maybe we'll be able to find some out there." She waved her hand toward the litter mixed in with the dead foliage and tree limbs. She thought she saw Kip's skateboard sticking out from under a pile of debris, but wasn't sure.

She heard the back door open and angled around. "Jared, I don't want you getting out."

Tears shone in his eyes. "Why not? We've got to look for our stuff."

"Tell you what. I'll check the area out and make sure it's safe and then you all can come over and go through everything. How about tomorrow?" Gideon started his Jeep.

Jared slammed the door closed. "What if it rains today?"

Kathleen bit her lower lip, her own tears making her vision blurry. "Hon, I don't think that will make a difference. If it's out there, it has survived a hurricane. A little rain won't hurt it. Everything we had can be replaced." Except the pictures and a few treasures, but she didn't want to say anything about them right now. It was hard enough seeing the destruction. "Let's go to Mom's."

Gideon sent her a reassuring smile. "I'll take care of it later today."

"I appreciate that." The sight of what was left of her cottage drained what little energy she had. The past two days had finally crashed down on her. All she wanted to do was sleep.

Later that afternoon as she awakened from a long nap, the scent of coffee brewing drifted to Kathleen. The aroma lured her to full alertness. She glanced at the battery-operated clock on the nightstand and bolted up in bed. Four o'clock. She hadn't wanted to sleep almost the entire day. Now she wouldn't get to sleep later tonight. That thought broke the dam on her emotions she'd kept reined in ever since she'd seen the destroyed cottage.

Her tears finally streamed down her face, flowing freely. Could things get any worse? Hope was devastated. The house she'd been living in was gone. She was drowning in debt her husband had accrued. Her sons were hurting emotionally. The tears turned to sobs that shook her. She drew her legs up against her chest and clasped them. For so long she'd been desperate to hold it together. Now she couldn't.

A soft knock at the bedroom door startled her. She tried to scrub away the evidence of her sorrow as she asked, "Who is it?" If it had been her sons, they would have burst into the room.

"Gideon."

She glanced down. Having no energy to change when she got home at ten-thirty this morning, she still wore her blue scrubs. As she swung her legs over the side of the bed, she continued to swipe at her tears.

"Are you all right?"

She stood—too fast. The room swirled before her eyes, still swimming with tears. "Yes. Be right there."

Steadying herself, she started for the door but caught sight of herself in the mirror. A gasp escaped her lips as she stared at the hollow look in her gaze staring back at her. Other than holing herself up in the bedroom, there'd be no way he wouldn't know she'd been crying. Inhaling several times, she opened the door.

He peered at her with an intensity that robbed her of the decent breath she'd just taken in. "Can I come in? I went by your house again while you were sleeping."

She stepped to the side and allowed him into her childhood bedroom, then shut the door. She didn't want her sons to overhear anything concerning the house. They already had enough to deal with.

"I'm glad I did. I found a nest of snakes under a pile of limbs and lots of boards with nails sticking up, but I think I've made the area safe enough for you and your sons. There are a lot of items among the debris that might be yours. It's hard for me to tell."

Kathleen sank down on her bed. "I don't want Jared or Kip going back there right now. I'll go over tomorrow and look around. They've lost so much. I don't want them to see their possessions destroyed. If I find any of their stuff, I'll bring it back."

"You know they won't like that. They've been very quiet today, but when they talk, they discuss what they're going to do when they go back home."

"Home?" The word came out on a shaky breath. Tears clogged her throat. She didn't want to cry in front of Gideon. She'd shed enough tears over the past year since her husband's death but always in private. "I don't know what that is anymore. When I came back to Hope, I felt this would be it. I wanted to make a home for my sons. I had hoped I could save enough money to buy the rental from Mom eventually. It was starting to feel like a home to me. Mom wanted to give me the cottage, but I wanted to make this work on my terms. This hurricane changed everything."

The overwhelming sense of loss suddenly hit her. She could no longer contain the sorrow. It swelled up and spilled down her cheeks.

Gideon put his arm around her and tugged her close to him. "You aren't alone."

Through the sobs, she mumbled, "I know the whole town feels that way right now." She swallowed hard, trying to tamp down her tears. What good did they do?

"No, I mean the Lord is with you through this. He is here to give us what we need."

"I need a home for Jared and Kip even if it is a two-bedroom house and they have to share a room. It was our home. We had one in Denver until it was repossessed and we had to move."

He tilted up her chin so their gazes connected. "Your home isn't a physical place. It's people. I know. I've been searching for one most of my life."

For a few seconds she thought she saw bleakness in his expression, but it vanished so quickly she wasn't sure. But he was hurting, too, and it had nothing to do with Hurricane Naomi. "What happened?"

"I lost my parents to a fire when I was eight. My brother and I were put in foster care and finally he was adopted. I wasn't. I had a lot of anger. Not your easiest child to handle. Zach's family moved away and over the years I've lost touch with him. He was five years younger than me and I couldn't keep us together. I blew it."

"Have you tried to find him?"

"Yes. I connected with him finally online about six months ago. He's serving in the marines and is overseas right now. I don't think he really remembers me. He was only four when he was adopted."

"I'm sorry. Don't give up on him."

"I'm not, but I'm not getting my hopes up that I'll suddenly have my brother back."

She came from a large extended family, many with roots around Hope. She couldn't image her life without them. Sniffing, she took his hand. "I know that my boys fight a lot, but they really love each other. If anyone threatened Jared, Kip would be there defending his brother and the reverse would be true. I've seen it happen right after they were yelling at each other."

"My family now is Station Two. The guys would do anything for each other. If Zach and I ever get together, fine, but I'm not counting on it."

"The people at the hospital are becoming an extended family to me. The way I've seen them coming together during this crisis awes me. Mildred—Nurse Ratched to you—is staying at the hospital. Mostly I think because she wants to let others stay home to help with their families. She doesn't have one. I hear she's always filling in during the major holidays so people can be with family."

He winced. "Okay, let's agree to forget my name for Mildred."

"I don't know. I may not let you live that one down."

"What can I do to change your mind?"

"Hmm. I'll have to think about that."

"When things calm down, I'll give Kip a grand tour of Station Two."

"You were already going to do that."

"A ride in a fire truck."

Kathleen tapped her chin with her forefinger. "Tempting. I'll keep that in mind."

Gideon rose and tugged her up, her body close to his. His masculine scent surrounded her, and the gleam in his eyes warmed her as the feel of his hand on her arm sent shivers down her spine. "I'm just gonna have to persuade you I'm one of the good guys."

He dipped his head toward her. Every nerve became alert, anticipating the meeting of their lips. Wanting it. She leaned toward him.

A knock sounded on the partially open door and her mother stuck her head through the opening. "I can't find Jared and Kip. They told me they were going upstairs to play in their room for a while. I went there to get them to do something for me and they aren't there. I've looked everywhere in the house and even in the yard. They're gone."

Chapter Seven

Kathleen quickly stepped away from Gideon. "Do you think they went to help someone in the neighborhood?"

"They've been helping the Johnsons but they've been good about letting me know and getting my okay." Ruth pushed the door open wide.

"Would they have gone back to the cottage?" Gideon headed for the hallway. "I can go look for them."

"They know never to leave the block without talking to me first or Mom and that is without a hurricane." Kathleen followed Gideon into the corridor.

"Gideon might be right about the cottage. I heard them whispering before they decided to go play in their room. That in itself should have been a red flag, but I've been cooking all afternoon so people on the block can have one hot meal a day. For a while they were helping me."

"Since this house is in the middle of the block, I'll go one way toward the cottage and you go the other," Gideon told Kathleen, then strode toward the front door. "We'll find them."

"Mom, you go on and finish cooking. Don't worry." Kathleen joined Gideon on the porch, the creases on her forehead deepening. "Now if only I could follow my own advice."

"Maybe they thought they could join me while I was over there. One of the neighbors helped and then I went to the fire station to see if there was anything I could do there. The boys wouldn't have known that."

"I'll go this way." Kathleen pointed east.

Gideon made his way to the end of the block and turned the corner, glancing back at Kathleen who'd been stopped by a neighbor. When he started down the street where the cottage was, he spied Kip out in front. He quickened his pace.

Kip looked up from digging through a pile of trash, grinned and waved at him. Hopping up, he yelled to Jared then ran down the middle of the road toward him. The boy's foot caught on a limb on the ground and he went flying forward, hitting the asphalt with a jolt.

Gideon rushed to the child, who had tears rapidly filling his eyes. Kip rolled over and held up his hands. They were bleeding. Gideon knelt next to him, noticing his jeans were torn at one knee. "Are you okay?" Taking Kip's hands, he examined the palms.

"It hurts."

"I know. It needs to be cleansed. Let me help you up."

The boy pushed up to a sitting position but didn't move any more than that. Suddenly he burst out crying and hugged his arms to his chest, rocking back and forth. For a moment Gideon didn't know what to do.

"Besides your hands, where else does it hurt?"

"Everything is gone. I can't find anything of mine."

Gideon settled his hand on Kip's shoulder. "You might not be able to. I know how hard that can be."

Kip looked up at him, his eyes shiny, tears coursing down his face. "But your house is all right."

"When I was about your age, my home burned down. Everything was destroyed. All I had was the clothes I had on when I escaped from the house."

Kip's gaze widened. "It did? What did you do?"

"Exactly what you did. I got upset. Then I grew very angry at the world. In the long run, that didn't help me at all. I pushed everyone away, even people who were trying to help me. I became so difficult that I ended up being moved from foster home to foster home. I never stayed in one place long. I was the one hurt by that."

"Like Mom moving here?"

"Not exactly. You still have your brother and mother. She will provide a home for you even if that means living with your grandmother. Y'all will be together."

Kip dropped his head and knuckled his eyes.

"I'm not gonna kid you. The next months will be hard. Everyone in Hope will have to pull together to put the town back even better than it was. You and your brother will have to do your part. The more united we are, the faster Hope will recover."

The child lifted his face, squaring his shoulders. "I can do my part."

"C'mon. Let's go get Jared. Your mom is worried about you two. She should be here shortly." Gideon rose and offered Kip his hand.

As the boy struggled to his feet, grimacing as he put weight on his leg with the torn jeans, Gideon saw Kathleen hurrying down the street toward them. A frown carved deep lines into her face.

"Kip, what happened?"

"I tripped, but I'm okay," he said in his tough-boy voice Gideon remembered using even while inside he'd been hurting.

"I found your skateboard," Jared shouted, holding it up.

"My skateboard!" Kip limped toward his little brother and took it from him. He turned and grinned at Gideon and his mother. "I didn't lose everything."

"How am I supposed to get angry at them when I see that?" Kathleen whispered, shifting toward him.

"Kip and I talked. They're scared. Everything familiar to them has been changing lately. They came over here to find anything of theirs they could cling to. I remember when I escaped the fire at my home, I grabbed my baseball card collection my dad and I started. It was my most prized possession."

"Do you still have it?"

Memories washed through him, sharpening the pain of loss. "At one of my foster homes someone stole it from me. I thought I knew who had it and started a fight with him. He didn't have it, but it got me thrown out of the house. It had been the last straw with the couple I lived with."

Kathleen covered her mouth and shook her head. "You never found it?"

"No. But no one can take away the memories I

have of my dad and me going to the store, deciding who to buy, putting it in a scrapbook."

Kathleen cleared her throat and turned back toward her children. "Do you mind if we take a little while to look around for the boys? Maybe there is something besides the skateboard."

"I was going to suggest that. At least until we find something of Jared's."

She threw him a grin as she moved toward her sons. "Or it gets dark."

"Good idea. Besides, your mother was determined to fix a big batch of spaghetti for everyone."

Kip heard Gideon. "Spaghetti! This day is getting better and better."

Kathleen stopped next to Jared. "Let's see what we can find of yours."

"Mom, I've looked everywhere. I don't think there is anything. At least I've got Bubbles at Nana's."

Gideon stood back for a few seconds while Kathleen and Jared went to a pile of items he'd stacked up earlier after clearing some debris and limbs away. These past few days had made him think about having a family. Years ago he'd given up on that idea. He'd been determined to go it alone in the world. But being with Kathleen and her sons revived that dream he'd had as a little boy. He'd been by himself for so long he didn't know if it were possible.

Half the neighborhood sat in her mother's living and dining rooms. Kathleen handed the last person to arrive a plate with spaghetti. Someone else had brought a premixed salad and another person had two loaves of French bread. As she scanned the faces of the people on the street, tired expressions met her perusal but each person gave her a smile.

When everyone was served and had a seat, her mother stood in the wide entrance between the two rooms and said, "I'd like to offer a blessing." After several people bowed their heads, she closed her eyes and continued, "Lord, I know You are here with us even if at times it doesn't seem like it. We need You. We need Your help rebuilding Hope. Bless this food we are sharing and the people who are gathered here. Amen."

A few around Kathleen murmured amen, but there were some people who grumbled. At the moment she didn't know what to feel. She fought the urge to shut down physically and mentally, but spiritually she was teetering on a ledge—ready to fall any second.

Gideon leaned toward her. "You okay?"

"Yeah, I'm still trying to sort out all my feelings. I feel like I'm at a boxing match and I'm down for the count. And it looks like most of the people are experiencing that, too."

"There's a lot to do in the coming months."

"Jared informed me earlier today that Christmas isn't too far away."

"The first of November is in a few days. I can't believe it."

"I think Jared wants to start a new rock collection. He was disappointed that he couldn't find it at the house."

"There's still more to go through. It might turn up."

"I'm not telling him that, or he'll get his hopes up. I don't want him to be any more disappointed than he was when we left the cottage this afternoon."

"What was it kept in? That way I'll know what to look for."

"It was in a wooden chest. He'd carved his name into it and about scared me to death. He'd gotten a hold of his dad's pocketknife. I wondered why he was so quiet. When I found him in his room, he had all but the 'd' carved in the box. Kip had helped him. The rocks are some we found on our hikes in Colorado." *When we were a family before the trouble started.* "He had a rock tumbler that polished them and made them shiny."

"And that's gone, too. That doesn't mean we can't collect rocks around here."

"He already has. He found one on the ground by the cottage and put it in his pocket."

"Kids have a way of bouncing back."

Kathleen chuckled. "Probably before us adults." Her gaze found Miss Alice sitting in a chair with a stool because her mother didn't have a recliner like Miss Alice was used to. "I hear she threatened to go home when she discovered there was no recliner here."

Gideon followed the direction of her look. "I fixed that stool for her. She calmed down after that."

"I imagine being here with Kip and Jared is a bit much for her. She never married and had children. I don't think she's been around very many."

Kip approached Miss Alice and said something to her. Handing Kip her plate, the older lady smiled, a dimple actually appearing in her wrinkled face. He darted away and threaded his way through the crowd as the neighbors finished and began standing.

"Mom told me that he's been trying to help her, whereas Jared is staying as far away from her as he can living in the same house."

Tom Baker, who lived across the street, stopped in front of Gideon. "Some of us are going to help remove the tree and cover the hole in Miss Alice's house tomorrow. The weatherman is saying there could be rain in a few days."

"Great. I want to help. What time?"

"We're thinking eight. It's gonna take a good part of the day. Her house is the worst one hit on the block."

"I'll be there."

Tom nodded at Gideon. "I figured you would say that. Do you have a chainsaw?"

"Yes."

"We'll need it."

"Is there anything I can do?" Kathleen asked.

Tom peered at her. "We could use some people to help haul the branches away."

"I can do that. Does Miss Alice know?"

The man stared down at the floor for a moment, dragging his hand through his hair. "I figured you could tell her. You two have a way with her."

Kathleen pressed her lips together to keep from laughing. Miss Alice's reputation was far worse than the woman really was. "I will."

"Good. We aim to help everyone on this street, even Miss Alice."

When he left, Gideon shifted toward her. "What about your house?"

"It's gone. There isn't much we can do now but look for some of our possessions. If we have time, we'll do it tomorrow afternoon."

"We? You mean Jared and Kip?"

"Yes, today I realized they need to do that. They

need some closure. We'll be staying at Mom's for a while. I think it will help them to understand the why of the tragedy by helping others and cleaning up the mess at the cottage."

"Besides, it will keep them out of trouble if they're working."

"Well, that, too. At least until school resumes."

"At the fire station I heard that might not be for a couple of weeks. Some of the schools sustained serious damage. The one on the Point flooded. They're going to have to find another place for the children to go to school—at least for most of the rest of the school year."

"Mom!"

A silence fell over the room at the sound of Jared's yell.

"Mom! Cottonballs is gonna eat Bubbles."

All gazes turned to her. She rose. Miss Alice struggled to sit forward in her chair.

"I'll take care of this, Miss Alice." Kathleen hurried from the room and up the stairs with Gideon following.

Upstairs in the room Kip and Jared shared at her Mom's, she found Jared holding a dripping wet white cat. Kathleen immediately looked at the goldfish, which was swimming around the bowl as though nothing had happened.

"He's a menace. We need to lock him up until he leaves." Jared's forehead was scrunched, his eyebrows slashing down. He held at arm's length a wiggling Cottonballs with his claws out, waiting to sink into something soft like flesh.

Gideon crossed the room and gingerly took the cat from Jared. The beast kept squirming, determined to get back to his food in the bowl. "I'll take him to Miss Alice."

After Gideon left, she shut the door and turned toward her son. "Let's keep this closed while Cottonballs is staying here."

"Why is he, Mom? Miss Alice is always frowning at me. She doesn't like me."

"Have you tried to talk to her?"

"Well, no. What do I say to her? She isn't like Nana. I've heard her yell at kids in her yard."

"I don't think she is used to kids."

"What do you mean?"

Kathleen sat on the twin bed nearest her. "She isn't around children much."

Jared gave her a confused look.

"Sometimes kids require a certain kind of patience not everyone has."

"I was thinking the same thing about Miss Alice."

"Hon, it won't be too long. Once her house is livable she'll want to leave. Put yourself in her shoes. She has always lived alone. Now all of a sudden she is living with two children and two adults. She knows Nana, but she really doesn't know us well. We're all family. She isn't part of our family and may be lonely. Maybe she feels left out a little. And she can't do much to help everyone with cleanup."

"Why not? She could help Nana fix the meals."

"You're right. I don't think anyone has asked her. But remember, Jared, she's a guest in our home."

"This isn't our home. It's Nana's. We don't—" His voice caught. "We don't have a home."

"Yes, we do. Home is where we are together even if it is at Nana's. We might not have a house or apartment for a while, but we have a home."

He cocked his head to the side. "Why can't we?"

"Because we were not the only ones who lost their house. There will be a shortage of places to live until people can rebuild. That will take time."

"Like Miss Alice's house?"

"Yeah. Her place will need extensive work to be livable again."

"While Nana's and Gideon's don't?"

"You're right. We only sustained minor damage compared to others." Kathleen shoved to her feet. "Now I need to go help Nana clean up. Are you coming downstairs?"

"No, I need to make sure Bubbles is all right."

Kathleen hugged Jared. "I love you. Everything will be all right in time."

As she left her sons' room and descended the steps to the ground floor, she wondered if everything really would be all right in time. She hoped—prayed—it would be, but she felt buried under a pile of rubble the storm created.

Seeing the house cleared of neighbors now that darkness was settling outside, Kathleen checked in the den where the sleeper sofa was set up for Miss Alice to see if she needed anything. The woman wasn't in the room. Voices coming from the kitchen drew her toward it. When she entered, she found Miss Alice drying the dishes while her mom washed and Gideon put them away in the cabinets.

"This is an efficient team. I guess you all don't need me."

Gideon slanted a look over his shoulder then continued to stack the glasses into the cupboard. "Yeah, we'll have this cleaned up in no time. Miss Alice was telling us about her first job when she was a young girl. She was a dishwasher in a fancy restaurant in New Orleans. I've eaten in the place a couple of times."

"You lived in New Orleans, Miss Alice? I thought you'd lived here all your life."

"Child, I lived all over the world until I was thirty and retired to Hope."

"Retired? At thirty?" Kathleen bridged the distance between them and made herself busy putting away the rest of the food.

"That's what I call it when I stopped traveling and put down roots in one place. I chose Hope for that."

"Why?" Gideon took the dried plate from Miss Alice.

"It was smaller fifty years ago, quaint and hospitable. I didn't want a big city where I didn't know many people. You might not believe this, but at one time I was a mover and shaker here in Hope. I've been through my share of hurricanes. I even organized groups to deal with the aftereffects here in town."

Kathleen shut the pantry door. "What did you do?"

"If people group together, the cleanup can go faster. A lot like what you've gotten this neighborhood to do, Ruth."

Her mother grinned at Miss Alice. "At your suggestion."

"Like what we're doing right now, cleaning up after dinner. Teamwork." Miss Alice's eyes twinkled as they fell on Gideon. "Like you do as a firefighter."

"It's hard fighting a fire without teamwork." Gideon put away the last dish.

What happened to Miss Alice while she was upstairs? Kathleen wondered. For the past couple of days, the old woman had been depressed and quiet but for now. Kathleen stared at her, trying to figure out the change.

Miss Alice caught her attention and winked. "It was Kip who reminded me I still have a lot to give. That I could still be part of the team."

Kathleen's mouth fell open, feeling as though the woman had read her mind.

"When Gideon brought Cottonballs downstairs a while ago, Kip hurried and took my cat, telling me he would take care of him. He knew I must be tired so I should rest. I suddenly realized that had been the way I had been acting for the past two days. No more. I may be eighty-six years young, but I'm not gone yet. So tomorrow I'll be at my house helping with whatever I can."

"You know what the neighbors are going to do?"

Miss Alice grinned. "Gideon broke the news to me. I may be set in my ways, but not that set, I can't appreciate the help." She folded the dish towel and shuffled toward the door that led into the hallway. "With that in mind, I need to get my sleep so I'll be ready. Good night. Ruth, the dinner was delicious."

When Miss Alice left, Kathleen swung her gaze between Gideon and her mother. "Is that the same lady who we kept over here during the storm and sat in a chair, not speaking or doing a thing for hours?"

"I've heard stories about Miss Alice in her younger days. She's right. She was a regular dynamo. Then about fifteen years ago she stopped going to church, being involved with others and holed herself up in her house. I was never sure why." Kathleen's mother started for the same exit. "I think I'll follow her. Good night."

Kathleen released a slow breath. "It's only eight but I feel like I've been up for the whole day instead of four hours."

"A lot has happened in that time."

"I'm tired but not sleepy."

"Me, too."

"Where did Kip go?"

"To feed Cottonballs and settle him in the laundry room. I guess I probably should also leave. I have some work I want to do at home."

"In the dark? We have your generator."

"I have lanterns like you do."

"Stay." The word came out before Kathleen could censure it, but she didn't want to be alone at the moment.

"I should— Okay, for a little bit."

Out of the corner of her eye, Kathleen saw a

flash dart by the doorway. "Why don't we go out on the porch so little boys with big ears don't eavesdrop?"

Gideon glanced toward the entrance and laid his forefinger over his mouth. "Surely you don't mean Jared or Kip?" he asked as he crept out of the kitchen through the dining room.

"Well, they have been known to listen when they shouldn't. You can never tell if..."

A roar erupted in the hallway followed by a yelp from Kip. Two seconds later her older son and Gideon came into the room.

"Look who I found standing by the door. Listening."

"Imagine that. My son with the big ears."

Kip frowned. "I don't have big ears. Jared does, but I don't."

"No, I don't," Jared squeaked from the dining room.

Kathleen made her way to where the sound came from and peeked around the door. "Come out. What were you doing behind there?"

Jared trudged into the kitchen, his eyes downcast. "If Kip can listen, so can I."

"Both of you need to get ready for bed. Now."

"But, Mom, it's only eight-twenty, and we don't even have school tomorrow." Kip's mouth twisted into a frown that he shot at his brother. "See what you made Mom do."

"I did not."

"Jared. Kip. Enough. We have a lot to do tomorrow, and we need to get up early. I don't want two cranky kids. That's why you're going to bed a little early. I understand from Nana you both were up late last night. You've got some sleep to make up."

"I don't need a lot of sleep. Besides, I shouldn't have to go to bed at the same time as Jared. I'm older. Age should have some privileges."

"I agree. And I'm older than both of you. So I get the privilege of you two listening to me then doing exactly what I say."

"But that's not what I meant."

"Go." Kathleen fluttered her hand toward the hallway.

"See you two tomorrow bright and early. I'm going to need two helpers. I can't do all I would like to do because of my cast." Gideon struggled to maintain a serious expression, but the second they disappeared into the hall, he chuckled.

"I heard that," Kip said right before he stomped up the stairs.

Gideon laughed even more. "Finally alone at last," he said to Kathleen.

"You think this will last? You don't know my boys. They'll come up with one excuse after another to come down here just so they can stay up."

He grabbed her hand and tugged her toward

the foyer. "Then let's escape onto the porch like you suggested."

"Great minds think alike."

As Kathleen shut the front door, she glimpsed Kip at the top of the stairs staring down at them. When he saw her, he turned around and went into his room.

The cool night air washed over Kathleen. She sat next to Gideon on the top step and surveyed the neighborhood. Dim lights, from candles and lanterns, shone from some of the houses, the only illumination on the street. The darkness hid the piles of debris and torn up landscape. Across from them, Tom Baker had a tarp over part of his roof covering a hole where some of the shingles had blown away. The place next to him had its carport ripped away from the house, pieces of it lying scattered all over the yards along the street.

The scent of salt water drifted to her, reminding her of how far the Gulf came ashore and covered the area near the beaches and swamped the whole peninsula known as the Point in Hope. The sea retreated but had left its mark on the town, the stench of dead fish and rotting vegetation.

Gideon laid his flashlight down beside him. "When I went to the station, I felt so useless. An alarm went off while I was there, and I had to stand by and watch the others leave to fight the fire."

"I'm so sorry. I'm the reason you're in that situation."

"Hold it. That isn't the reason I told you that. You're not to blame for my injury. I thought we were past that. What do I have to do to make you understand that?"

Her husband had always made her feel she was the cause of things that had gone wrong in their marriage. As though she had been the one to get them into debt. She'd begun to wonder if she was the reason. Had Derek thought she'd wanted a new car or a swimming pool? She hadn't, but he'd acted as if she had.

"Old habits die hard." Placing her elbows on the tops of her thighs, she leaned forward and clasped her hands.

"What do you mean?"

"According to my husband, I was the reason everything went wrong." She turned toward him and realized how close he was to her on the step. Their arms brushed against each other. His coffee-laced breath mingled with the night scents. Her heartbeat reacted to his nearness by speeding up. "Don't get me wrong. I know marriage is a two-way street. We rushed into it. I think I was in love with the idea of marriage. I won't make that mistake again."

"What mistake?"

"Marrying. The year before Derek died I felt like I had to guard everything I said. I even went to the doctor because I was so anxious. I would cry at the drop of a hat. I was always so tired, and it wasn't from work like it is now. My husband didn't want me to work after Kip was born. I agreed with him." *To keep the peace.*

Gideon covered her hands with his. "You'll feel different with time. It hasn't been that long since he passed away."

She nodded. "Fifteen months. But I don't think time will make a difference."

"You're a great mother, patient with your sons even when they test you. You might want to marry again, have another child. Your mom told me you once said you wanted six kids."

"I was fourteen. When did she tell you that?" She was going to have to keep an eye on her mother. Next she would be bringing out her baby pictures to show Gideon. She knew what her mom was up to, and she needed to put a stop to it.

"When she was quizzing me about when I was going to start a family. I don't think your mother knows the meaning of the word subtle."

"I'm finding that out lately. Don't mind her. She thinks the answer to my problems is a man. She doesn't understand a man got me into the mess I'm in." The second she said that her cheeks flamed, heat radiating down her neck. "I mean…"

His hold on her cupped hands tightened as he shifted toward her. "Shh. I understand perfectly."

In the soft glow she could barely make out his face. But she couldn't read the expression on it. Which meant he couldn't read hers. Relief trembled through her because embarrassment still heated her cheeks. The cool breeze flowed over her, but it did little to ease the warmth suffusing her.

"This past week you and your family have kept me sane. You have given me a purpose at a time when I haven't been feeling so useful. You have to understand I'm a man of action. That came to a grinding halt with the accident."

She opened her mouth to tell him she was sorry again, but he covered her lips with his fingers.

"Not a word about you causing it or I will leave."

"Do you always threaten friends?" She tried to school her voice into a serious tone, but laughter leaked through.

"I'm not answering that on the grounds that it might incriminate me." He cradled her face in his large palm. "When do you go back to the hospital?"

"The day after tomorrow. I think we'll be back on our regular schedule soon unless something further happens. How about you? When do you report to headquarters for desk duty?"

He groaned. "Don't remind me. In two days, but I guess it's better than doing nothing."

The feel of his skin against hers momentarily robbed her of speech. She frantically tried to put together a coherent sentence, but every inch of her was aware of the man sitting next to her, so close his breath fanned her chin. "You call what you've been doing nothing, and you've been doing it with only one arm. I certainly have appreciated all your hard work around here and at the cottage."

"I'm glad." He bent a few more inches toward her, their mouths only a breath away.

Her pulse accelerated. Her throat went dry. Her stomach tightened.

His hand ran down her jawline until he took hold of her chin and tilted it up toward him. Her lips parted as she inhaled deeply.

Chapter Eight

All evening Gideon had wanted to kiss Kathleen, so when his lips touched hers, it felt right. Better than right. He wound his arm around her and drew her to him. His mouth settled on hers as he deepened the kiss, pouring into it all the feelings he'd experienced whenever he was near her. Earlier, he'd watched her mouth move as she talked, smiled or frowned. He'd wondered what it would feel like when his moved over hers. Now he knew.

But in the back of his mind he heard Kathleen's words again. She didn't want to become involved with any man. She'd been burned by her deceased husband. She had been warning him. And he needed to listen.

When she slid her arms around his neck, he pulled back, his ragged breath sounding in the sudden quiet of night. "I'd better be going."

Pushing to his feet, he hovered over her. She peered up at him, but he didn't want to see her expression. He wanted to think she enjoyed the kiss, at least some. But he also needed to remember she didn't want to get involved with a man. He had lost too many special people in his life. There was no way he would go through that kind of pain again. So he had to back off before he fell in love and ended up hurt.

"Good night. I'll see you tomorrow." He descended the remaining two steps, wanting to stay and pursue the feelings rampaging through him, but needing to go because of those feelings. He pivoted and started down the sidewalk.

"Gideon."

He stopped and turned but he didn't say anything. No words would describe the conflict raging in him.

"I— Thank you for your help today."

"Anytime." This time he rotated around and hurried away.

Kathleen watched Gideon almost flee from her. What just happened?

She ran her fingers across her lips. *I was kissed by a dynamite, caring man. I was...*

She didn't know what to think. Instead, she sat there letting her feelings dominate her—no, overwhelm her. From her hammering heartbeat to the tingling awareness of everything about Gideon.

What made him stop and pull away?

Did I do something wrong?

Derek's rejections the last year and a half of their marriage mocked her. Would she ever be free of those memories?

She stood, pulling in deep breaths over and over to calm her. She hadn't come to Hope to find a man. She didn't believe, like her mother, that a man was the solution to her problems. A man had put her into debt, attacked her self-confidence. No, she would be fine by herself. She would put her family back together.

But still she had wanted that kiss to continue. She'd wanted to bask in the feeling of femininity it had brought out in her for a while longer.

The next evening after spending the day at Miss Alice's and then at the cottage picking through the rubble, Kathleen helped her mother put together soup and sandwiches. The back door opened and in came Jared.

"Did you two invite Gideon to dinner?" her mother asked as she put the soup onto the stove to heat.

"Yep. He's going home to wash up and feed Butch. Kip went with him."

"He did?" Kathleen needed to say something to Kip about bugging Gideon too much.

"He wanted to help with Butch." Jared's gaze lit upon Miss Alice sitting at the kitchen table.

"Whatcha doing, Miss Alice?" Jared plopped himself down across from the older woman, put his elbow on the tabletop and settled his chin in his palm.

"I had to do something. Your mom and grandma didn't want me to help with dinner so I'm playing solitaire."

"Can I watch?"

"Sure, if that floats your boat."

"Floats my boat? I don't have one."

Miss Alice laughed. "If that makes you happy."

"Nana plays solitaire sometimes, but it doesn't look like that."

"There are hundreds of different kinds of solitaire."

"Why don't they have different names?"

"Solitaire really means any card game you can play by yourself."

"Oh."

"Why didn't you go with your brother?"

"I don't know." Jared shrugged. "I guess 'cause I'm tired after working all day."

"You did good."

Jared beamed. "I did?"

"Both you and Kip really helped Gideon. I heard him say so. I just wish I could have done more."

"But you're an old lady."

"Jared!" Kathleen closed her eyes and waited for Miss Alice's reaction.

"And proud of it. I've seen and done many things." A chuckle accompanied her declaration.

"Like what?" Jared moved around to the seat next to Miss Alice to watch her play the card game.

"I've ridden a camel in the desert and an elephant in India. I've dived with sharks, and I've climbed some of the tallest mountains in the world."

His eyes grew round. "Weren't you scared the sharks would eat you?"

"Tell you a secret." Miss Alice leaned close and whispered something in Jared's ear.

Kathleen didn't think her son's eyes could get any bigger. "The first time! How many times did you swim with them?"

"Half a dozen times. I'll show you some of my pictures when I can get back into my house."

"I'd like that."

"Now let me show you how to play this version of solitaire." Miss Alice shuffled the deck and laid the cards down in a pyramid, telling Jared what she was doing as she did it.

When Kathleen heard a knock on the front

door, she merely continued making the sandwiches. Her mother looked over at her and said, "That must be Gideon. Would you answer the door?"

Kathleen thought about refusing her mother's request, but that would start a whole series of questions she didn't want to answer. Besides, she and Gideon could be casual friends.

She finished cutting the last turkey and Swiss cheese sandwich in half, then hurried into the foyer. Gideon stood on the porch. A picture of him kissing her the night before flashed into her thoughts—along with an image of him ending it suddenly and leaving right after that. All day she had avoided being near him and now she was face-to-face with him, only two feet from him. Way too close for her peace of mind.

He had kissed her and found her lacking. The insecurity she experienced reminded her of Derek that last year of their marriage. He had hardly ever touched her.

"Where's Kip?" Her voice cool, she stepped to the side to let him into the house.

"Butch needed walking, and he wanted to do it. I said okay. I hope that's all right with you."

"That's fine."

She swept around to go back into the kitchen, but Gideon grasped her hand and stopped her. "Is something wrong?"

Yes. His warm touch only reinforced his rejection. "No, everything is fine."

"I'll go get Kip. I shouldn't have let him do it." He released her hand and started to open the door.

"Leave Kip. I said it was fine. I know how much my children love animals."

"Then this must be about last night. You've hardly said two words to me today. I know I shouldn't have kissed you. I was presuming something between us that's not there."

Being punched in the stomach would be better than what she was feeling right now. She backed away. She gritted her teeth and tried to think of something elegant to say. Nothing came to mind except all the hurt his words produced.

"I'm not explaining myself well. I mean—"

"Please, you've made yourself quite clear. Now, if you'll excuse me, I need to help Mom get dinner on the table."

This time he didn't stop her from leaving. Thankful he hadn't, she fought the tears jamming her throat. All she wanted to do was get through this evening without saying or doing something she would regret.

In the kitchen, her mother studied her for a few seconds then went back to setting out the paper goods they were using so they didn't have as much to wash. "Dinner is ready." She looked behind Kathleen. "Where's Kip?"

In the doorway Gideon replied, "I'll go see what's keeping him." Then he disappeared down the hallway before anyone could say anything.

The sound of the front door opening and closing filled the quiet.

Miss Alice swung her attention from Kathleen to her mom, then rose and asked Jared, "Will you help this old lady to the restroom to wash her hands?"

Jared jumped up and held Miss Alice's arm.

"We'll be gone for a few minutes," she announced as she and Jared left the kitchen.

Her mom leaned back against the counter. "Okay. What's going on? I noticed all day you didn't say anything to Gideon. Are you two having a fight?"

"That would imply there was something between us."

One of her mother's eyebrows rose. "And there isn't?"

"No, we're barely friends."

"Oh, I see. So you two did have a fight."

"No, we didn't and I don't care to talk about this anymore. I'm starved. I worked up quite an appetite today."

"Ignoring your feelings will not make them go away. Since you and Gideon were getting along so well yesterday, I guess something happened after

I went to bed last night. Today you wouldn't even think y'all knew each other. What happened?"

The tears fought to be released. Kathleen swallowed again and again. "On second thought, I'm not very hungry. I have to be at work at seven tomorrow. I'm turning in early tonight." Biting her lower lip to keep from crying, she headed for the hallway.

"But, honey, it's only six."

She ignored her mother's words and rushed up the stairs before Gideon returned with Kip. She didn't want to run into him. She didn't understand what she was going through, but she was determined to get a handle on it before she saw him again.

In the safety of her bedroom, she closed the world out and sank onto her bed. What happened last night was a good thing. It reconfirmed that she didn't need to get involved with anyone. Maybe after her children were grown up, when what occurred between her and a man would only affect her. Her sons didn't need to be subjected to a volatile situation as they were the past few years no matter how much she tried to protect them. Jared and Kip needed stability. That needed to be her focus.

A rap at her door startled her. "Who is it?"

"Gideon. May I talk to you?"

No, she wanted to shout, but instead she closed her eyes, fortified herself with a lungful of air and rose. Her pace slowed as she neared the door, and when she opened it, she still wasn't prepared to see him. Nor the angry expression on his face.

"Can I come in?" Steel accompanied each word.

She backed away and let him into her bedroom.

She opened her mouth to speak, but he cut her off. "I asked you if there was anything wrong and you kept telling me everything was fine. Friends don't do that to each other."

"Friends. Is that what we are?"

"Yes." He paused and averted his gaze for a moment. "At least that was what I thought."

"And so friends kiss each other like we did last night?"

"I knew it. I knew I shouldn't have kissed you. I've ruined everything, and I didn't want to do that."

"Wow. That certainly makes me feel better. You regret kissing me."

"I never said that. I shouldn't have kissed you because it led to complications, and I don't want to lose your friendship."

"That's nice to know."

"Sarcasm doesn't become you."

She closed the space between them, her own anger surging to the surface. "Tell me why you kissed me last night. What were you trying to prove?"

"All day I'd been thinking about kissing you, and I thought if I did, that would be it."

She sucked in a ragged breath. "I guess I should appreciate your honesty." But her self-confidence had taken a beating the past couple of years. She hadn't realized how much until he'd pulled away and left so quickly the night before.

"You want honesty?" He got in her face.

She stood her ground. "Yes."

"After you said that you weren't interested in getting involved with anyone, I had decided that was fine. I could respect your wishes. Then before I realized it I was kissing you, telling myself that at least I could satisfy my curiosity then let it go."

"I'm so glad I could accommodate you. Now you won't lose any sleep over that."

A humorless laugh escaped his lips. "I wish that were the case."

"What do you mean? You pulled away and left in such a hurry I wasn't even sure what had happened. I figured you regretted—" She stopped, realizing what she was revealing.

"If you were going to say I regretted kissing you, you're right."

Her anger dissolved into hurt with his declaration.

"And you are wrong."

"What do you mean?"

"I mean that kiss was amazing, but after what you said I shouldn't have done it. I should have respected your wishes and not complicated our relationship. I'm sorry I didn't communicate that well to you last night or earlier this evening."

"The kiss was amazing?"

He looked at her for a long moment then grinned. "Most definitely. Everything I anticipated and more."

The words washed away the hurt and lifted her spirits. "I thought—"

He held up his hand. "No more speculation. If something is wrong, we need to talk it out. That is what friends do. You and your family have made my medical leave bearable, and I appreciate that more than you can know."

"I guess this isn't the time to point out I was the reason for the medical leave."

A stern look descended. "This is the last time I am going to speak of this." He rapped his knuckles against his hard cast. "I forgive you. Totally. One hundred percent."

Kathleen chuckled. "Okay. I believe you. I promise."

"It's about time. Because I didn't know what else I could do or say to convince you. I guess I could have had my friend write it in the sky for the whole town to see."

"Don't you dare." Laughter overtook her as she pictured the words. *Kathleen, you are forgiven. Gideon.* "That would set the tongues wagging in

Hope. I probably wouldn't be able to show my face. Of course, it would take everyone's mind off the hurricane."

"Well, then I'll do that."

She punched him playfully in the arm. "You'd better not."

"I won't. I don't want to get on your bad side again."

A shriek and barking reverberated through the house. Kathleen started for the door. "Kip brought Butch back here?"

"Well, not exactly."

"I'm not sure I want to hear what you mean by that."

"That will depend."

Kathleen opened the door and stepped out into the hallway at the same time a small brown wiry-haired dog ran down it with Cottonballs on its tail. Kip raced after the pair toward the living room.

"*That* is what it depends on?" Kathleen gestured toward the dirty dog.

"Yep. How do you feel about adopting a homeless dog?"

Kip skidded to a stop at the end of the corridor and swept around toward her. "I found him hiding under a bush. He was scared, shaking and whining. He's lost. I had to bring him home." Then before she could reply, he hurried down the stairs after the fighting animals, drawn no doubt by the racket the mutt and Cottonballs were causing in the living room.

"I'm not sure this is the best time. I never got to have a dog when I was younger. Mom didn't want any pets." Kathleen entered the living room to the picture of Kip kneeling by the couch and trying to coax the dog out from under it while Cottonballs stood next to him, tail puffed out, teeth bared and giving off a banshee cry that made *her* hair stand up.

Miss Alice, Jared and her mom came into the room from the kitchen.

Kip lifted his head, looked at Kathleen and said, "Mom, he is so scared. Do something," then went back to trying to soothe the animal.

"Jared, can you get Cottonballs and take him to the laundry room for me?" Miss Alice moved slowly toward the sofa while Jared darted around her and scooped up the cat that continued to hiss and scream as he took him away. Miss Alice trailed after Jared.

Her mom stepped over to the sofa. "What's going on here? What is under there? Another cat?"

Gideon inched closer to Kathleen and whispered, "Kip brought the dog in through the front door and was taking him upstairs when Cottonballs sensed his territory had been invaded and went on the defensive. I didn't have a chance to say anything to your mom."

Kathleen stooped next to Kip and leaned down until she saw the mutt cowering in the back. On closer inspection the dog appeared underfed. His ribs showed, and that sight squeezed her heart. "Maybe if we moved the couch, he'll come to you, Kip."

"What's going on?" Ruth asked again. "What's under there?"

Kip peered up at his grandmother. "I found a dog that needs a home. Can I keep him? Please."

"I don't know if that is such a good idea. I'm not a pet person."

"But, Nana, he's homeless. We can't turn him away. We've got Cottonballs here. He's a pet, and Gideon had Butch here during the hurricane. Pretty please."

"But that's the reason why. We do have Cotton-balls here. One pet is enough. Look what nearly happened with Bubbles."

"No one will know he's here. I'll keep him in my room. Feed him. Bathe him. Walk him. Besides, Miss Alice will be leaving soon when her house is fixed up."

Her mother sent Kathleen a beseeching look.

"Honey, let's get him out from under the couch first. Gideon, will you help me move it?"

"Sure. Kip, be ready to snatch him if he makes a run for it."

Kathleen stood on one end of the sofa while Gideon took the other. "One, two, three. Lift."

Positioned to grab the mutt when the couch was moved, Kip lunged forward and scooped up the medium-size dog, skinny with his ribs showing. "See. He's been homeless for a while and he has no collar."

"It's dirty." Her mother wrinkled her nose and backed away. "He needs to be outside. We don't have enough water yet to bathe him."

"I can't keep him?"

"Certainly not in this house until he is clean. No telling what he's brought in here. Fleas. Ticks." Her mother folded her arms over her chest.

"I don't have to drink any water. He can have my share."

Kathleen's gaze fastened onto the dog's sad face as he laid his head on Kip's shoulder. The animal's brown eyes latched on to hers. "Mom, why don't we keep him in the garage for right now? At least for the time being while we decide what to do with him."

"Please, Nana. I promise he won't be a problem."

"Fine, for now. But you have to do everything for it. And you have to keep it away from Cottonballs. I thought an animal was dying in here."

"Thanks. I will. You'll see."

Gideon scratched the animal behind his ears. "C'mon. I'll help you set up a bed for him. We'll make him feel right at home in the garage."

Kip rushed past his grandmother as though he was afraid she would change her mind.

Which given a chance, she might. Kathleen closed the gap between her and her mother. "Thanks. This means a lot to Kip."

"It stays only as long as it isn't any problem. We don't know what kind of diseases it carries. It's so mangy looking."

"I think some food will help with that, and I'll have a vet look him over. The dog must have been on his own for some time. Probably before the hurricane. He looks like he hasn't eaten much lately."

"So what do we feed him? I don't have any dog food here."

"I'll talk with Gideon. Don't worry." She hugged her mother then headed toward the garage.

Kip found an old comforter in the Goodwill bag her mother kept and put it down near the door into the house. When he set the dog on it, he stroked the dirty fur on the animal's back and murmured, "You're all right now. I'm gonna take care of you."

"How about food?" Kathleen asked as the dog curled into a ball, laying his head on Kip's leg.

"I can get some of Butch's dog food. I stocked

up when the hurricane was coming. He'll need a bowl of water, too."

Kip grinned up at Gideon. "Thanks. He needs a lot of it."

"I'll find a bowl and fill it with water." Kathleen snagged Gideon's attention. "May I have a word with you?"

He nodded and backed toward the door into the house.

"Mom, tell Nana it's my share of the water."

"We'll find a way for everyone to have water, even your dog. I think the water will be restored soon anyway, so we'll be fine."

"See, I told you everything would be okay." Kip put his arm around the mutt and rubbed his face against the matted, dirty fur.

Kathleen hurried inside before she threw herself between the dog and her son. *Boys like to get dirty. Boys like to get dirty.*

In the kitchen she shifted toward Gideon. "Which vet do you take Butch to? I hope he can see Kip's dog tomorrow."

"Dr. Anderson. Let me see if his clinic is set up to receive patients. The area of town it's in didn't get hit as hard as some. When are you off work tomorrow?"

"I should be home by four."

"We can do that, then stop by the beach afterwards."

"Why?"

"It's not the most ideal bathtub to bathe an animal in, but it's better than nothing."

"Good thinking."

"I'll have everything set up tomorrow for the dog. You can go to work and not worry about it."

As he left the kitchen, Kathleen began searching for a bowl for the water. When pulling down a plastic dish to use, she stopped in midmotion. In a short time she was beginning to depend on Gideon, to turn to him for help with certain problems. She had to put a halt to that or she would fall right back into the role she had in her marriage where she'd let Derek run everything. She really had only herself to blame for the situation she'd found herself in. She'd never insisted to be informed about their finances. Their marriage had never been a partnership, and she just now realized she was partially the reason it hadn't been.

Chapter Nine

Kathleen surveyed the live oak that remained standing guard near the old white lighthouse on the Point. From what she understood, the historical tree, more than two hundred fifty years old, would live in spite of the fact the hurricane had stripped off all its leaves. Seeing it gave her hope that the town would revive and be better than ever. The Peace Oak, as it had been known through history, had been where a treaty had been signed between the French and the Indians in the area.

Gideon came up behind her and stopped next to her, staring at the lighthouse. "It makes me feel good to see these two landmarks here after the surge of water covered most of the Point."

The past two weeks she and Gideon had seen each other in passing and a couple of times had stopped to talk but that had been all. With the power and water back on, most of the neighbors had retreated to their own houses to repair what they could. She missed the camaraderie of working on a team. "The lighthouse definitely needs a fresh coat of white." Four feet up the structure all the paint was gone and above that band the rest was dull from years of wind and weather.

"That's one of the projects we are tackling today. If we can get the park back into some kind of order, then we'll be able to decorate it for Christmas."

"So they'll still turn the holiday lights on Thanksgiving evening?"

"Yep, twelve days away. That's why we're here. The powers-that-be want the holidays to be like every other year."

"Actually, that's a smart move." Kathleen pointed toward the Peace Oak. "Now if we could glue the leaves back on it, it would be like every other year."

"Gotta find those leaves first."

"They're probably somewhere around Jackson." She turned away from the tree and lighthouse and scanned the beehive of activity all around Broussard Park that was one of the favorite spots for the townspeople. "So what are you doing here today?"

"Helping rebuild the playground. Zane Davidson is donating the new equipment along with some help setting it up." He nodded toward a large truck pulling into the parking lot. "In fact, he's here with it now. What are you doing?"

"Helping to lay gravel for the playground."

"Ah, so we'll be working together. Since Miss Alice's house, I've missed that."

For the past two weeks she had been pulling double duty at the hospital, coming home and helping her mother repair what they could or going to the cottage to dig through the debris for anything of hers or her sons'. "I'm almost through with the cleanup at the cottage. The city should be around at the end of the week to pick up the trash."

"Where are Jared and Kip?"

"Coming later with Mom and Miss Alice. They're contributing lunch for the volunteers."

"Good. I've arranged for your sons to tour Station Two next Saturday. I want to tell them today, but I want your okay first."

"They'll enjoy it."

"How's Rocky doing?"

"The second Kip was able to give him a bath he started bugging Mom about letting him come in and stay in his room. I think he's been counting down the days until Miss Alice goes back to her house. Davidson's Construction Company will be starting on her home Monday. Do you know Zane is only charging her whatever the insurance company gives her to repair her home? She won't even have to pay the thousand dollar deductible. When Zane told her that, I thought for a moment Miss Alice was going to do a jig."

"Now that I would have liked to see."

"I went to school with Zane, and if you had told me he would be doing so much for Hope, I would have scoffed at that."

Gideon's forehead crunched. "Why? Since he returned to Hope, he's been doing a lot for the town."

"When he was in high school, he had quite the reputation of being the bad boy. He rode a motorcycle way too fast and drank. But when I saw him at Miss Alice's house yesterday, I hardly recognized him."

Gideon waved at a tall, black-haired man talking to the driver of the truck.

"You know him?"

"Yeah, this past year he's been coming to this park to play basketball with my youth group."

"What's going to happen to Hope Community Church?" She glanced toward the church across the street from the park. All that remained of the front building was the bell tower. The older original church that had stood behind the newer part was still intact, not having received any water damage because it sat on a rise that had protected it from the flooding.

"We have plans to restore the worship area in the original church. The pastor hopes to have it complete by Christmas Eve services, even if the rest of the church restoration hasn't been done. It amazes me how the building built a hundred and fifty years ago withstood the hurricane but not the one built seventy years ago."

"Have you ever wondered why certain things happen while others don't? Like the church or the tree falling on Miss Alice's house. It could have fallen on Mom's."

"That's why I've always felt being prepared for everything is better."

"But you can't always think of everything. Events occur out of the blue that throw your life into a tailspin."

"Is that what happened when your husband died? He had to be young."

She nodded. "Thirty-five. That's young for a heart attack, but he had been under a great deal of stress. He'd tried to hide the trouble he was in, and it had taken its toll on his body."

"What kind of trouble?"

"Financial. He got himself into debt. He took a second mortgage out on the house. When he died, I couldn't make the payments. The bank foreclosed on us. I tried to stay in Denver for the boys. So much had changed in their lives, I didn't want to move away from what they were familiar with. I sank deeper into debt. Finally, I came home."

"And now with the hurricane, you've lost what you had when you came back to Hope?"

"Yes. Some pieces of furniture and boxes of possessions were still at Mom's, but most of what we owned was in the cottage. I hadn't gotten renter's insurance yet. All we have from the cottage fits in two boxes."

He moved close and took her hands. "But you and your sons are alive."

"Yes, and my car was at Mom's so it wasn't a total loss."

"Many people are in the same predicament. We just have to pull together. One prayer is good, but when it can be many, that's even better."

As before, Gideon's nearness sent her pulse racing. Her senses became attuned to him, everything else fading into the background. As far as she was concerned, they were alone in the park. The breeze from the Gulf carried the scent of the sea. The warmth of the sun canceled out the slight chill in the wind. It was a perfect day, a day to enjoy a picnic, like when she was a child.

"Mom!" Jared ran across the parking lot toward her.

Life intruded. Kathleen tugged her hand from Gideon's and stepped back, turning toward Jared

and smiling. This wasn't a day to enjoy a picnic.
It was a day of work, a day to remember what
happened in Denver with her husband. A day to
remind herself not to rush into anything, to be
cautious.

"I helped Miss Alice and Nana with the sandwiches. Kip didn't. He was playing with Rocky."
Jared skidded to a stop in front of her. "Nana told
me to tell you her and Miss Alice are setting up
over by the bell tower." Facing Gideon, he stood
at attention. "What can I do? I'm here to help.
Nana said we have to if we want a playground."

Gideon clasped his hand on Jared's shoulder.
"Let's go see what we can do."

She watched her son walking off with Gideon,
both with casts on their left arms. The sight thick-
ened her throat. Often when she was working and
Gideon was off, her sons spent time with him,
helping around his house or a neighbor's. Butch
and Rocky had become "best buddies" according
to Kip.

Jared stopped and whirled around. "Aren't ya
coming?"

"Yes," she answered, noticing Kip helping her
mother carry the food to the church.

If she could ignore the damage all around her,
she could for a moment see a glimmer of hope.
Jared and Kip had settled in at her mother's. She

had a good job, which would help her get back on her feet. She was surrounded by family and friends who cared. But she knew this moment would never last. Worry nibbled at her composure. She kept waiting for the other shoe to fall.

Zane approached Gideon. "You're determined to ignore that cast on your arm, aren't you?"

He laughed. "I keep trying to get my captain to ignore it."

"Obviously desk duty isn't setting well with you."

"Would it with you? You own a large construction company, and yet I see you often working at one of your sites. How come?"

"I enjoy it. Hard work makes me feel alive."

Gideon stared at his friend he'd met while trying to put out a grass fire threatening the pine forest along Interstate 10, all because someone had thrown out a lit cigarette. "It's scary how alike you and I are."

"That's why I want to know what is going on between you and Kathleen. I knew her in high school. She was a freshman when I was a senior. Nice girl."

"She's a nice woman."

Zane cocked an eyebrow. "Don't tell me you're abandoning me. I thought we would go into old age as confirmed bachelors."

"How did you get *nice woman* to mean marriage? I think all this hard work is going to your head."

"In all the years I've known you, I haven't heard of you dating a woman longer than a couple of weeks. Long-term isn't in your vocabulary."

"And it is in yours?"

"No," Zane said with a chuckle.

"For your information, three years knowing me isn't that long. I've dated women longer than two weeks."

"Who?"

Gideon stuck up his forefinger. "One is Missy Collins, two is…" He could hardly even count Missy because they were more friends than anything else.

"Two?"

"Okay, I haven't found the right one yet." And most likely wouldn't since he wasn't looking for any long-term commitment.

"So this makes Kathleen special."

"Of course she's special, but we haven't even gone out on one date."

"From what I've heard from Pete, you're always over at her mother's. He said something about arranging a tour of the station for her sons. I just saw you a while ago having an intense conversation with her. It looks serious to me."

Gideon released a frustrated breath. "You're

not going to rile me. Since when have you listened to gossip?"

"Pete seemed to think it might be something."

"Since when have you listened to Pete?"

"Since high school. Why haven't you gone out on a date?"

"Hurricane Naomi. Did you forget about that?"

"Not all dates are at a restaurant, the movies or something like that."

"Now you're giving me dating advice?"

Zane clapped him on the back. "Someone's gotta help you. That's what a friend is for—giving you unsolicited advice. I'm quite good at it."

Gideon gestured toward a worker. "I think one of your men needs your unsolicited advice."

"I think I've treaded on a touchy subject."

"Bye, Zane."

His friend's laughter as he strode toward his worker grated on Gideon's nerves. Why would he risk getting hurt after Kathleen made it clear she wasn't interested? But Zane was right. They didn't have to go to a restaurant for a date, and friends could go out together. Kathleen deserved something special. She'd been working nonstop since the hurricane. Maybe he could do something about that—as a friend.

"Hey, Gideon, we're taking a break. Wanna shoot some hoops?" Kip approached him with a basketball under his arm. "I got this from the church. Nana said it would be all right to take it so long as I put it back."

"Sure. Let's see if we can get some other boys and maybe a couple of dads."

Kip turned in a slow circle, going from one father and son to another. A frown creased his forehead.

It didn't take much for Gideon to figure that Kip was missing his dad. He could remember the first few times after his dad had died and he'd seen a father and son together how much it had hurt him to realize he would never have that. He'd gotten really good at avoiding situations where that might take place. The hurt had faded but never totally went away.

"Trust me," Gideon said the next Friday and turned Kathleen away from him. "Close your eyes. I'm putting a blindfold on you."

"Blindfold? Why?"

"It's a surprise and I don't trust you will keep your eyes closed."

"Do you hear yourself? You ask me to trust you and yet—" The feel of the cloth over her eyes interrupted her train of thought. Actually it was more the close proximity of Gideon and the lime-scented aftershave she smelled that affected her thinking.

He leaned near her ear and whispered, "And yet I don't trust you to keep your eyes closed? Sometimes life doesn't make sense."

"More like you don't make sense," she said in response to him but was amazed she managed to utter those words when she still felt the tickle of his breath on her neck. She pictured him nibbling on her lobe and nearly melted into her mother's front lawn.

He chuckled. "I've been told that before. Now quit complaining and relax. You've been working too much lately."

"And you haven't?" He took her hand and led her to his Jeep.

"I have called in a few favors to pull this together so I want you to sufficiently appreciate my efforts."

"But there is so much to do."

"I agree and it will be there tomorrow. Have you taken any time for yourself in the past three weeks since the hurricane?"

"Are you kidding? With the cleanup and the demands at the hospital? Just yesterday a man came in who was trying to repair his own roof and fell off. He broke several ribs, and one punctured his lung." She relaxed back against the seat while he pulled out of the driveway.

"When the power came back on, we had several electrical-caused fires. It's bound to happen with all the damage."

"We take for granted electricity until we lose it. So much of what we use is run by electricity and without it, we become lost."

"One good thing was the hurricane was late in the season and the temperature wasn't as unbearable as it can get in the summer."

"Or cold like in Denver, even in November."

Gideon slowed down then made a right turn. Kathleen tried to figure out by the direction he drove where he was taking her, but she wasn't as familiar with Hope as she had been growing up and with the hurricane, detours were necessary in some places. Sections of the road along the coast were still closed off because of extensive damage to the pavement.

When he stopped, he opened the door and said, "Stay right there. Don't take off the blindfold. I'm coming around to lead you to my surprise."

She was tempted to peek but then decided to give in to what Gideon was doing. He'd gone to some trouble to do this, and she didn't want to disappoint him. He'd done a lot for her family. Jared and Kip were constantly making excuses to go down and see Gideon. She'd even found herself trying to come up with one, especially since the day at Broussard Park. Seeing Gideon playing basketball with her sons made her realize how much anger she still had toward Derek. It should have been him, but he'd chosen a destructive path. He'd wanted possessions over his family.

When Gideon opened her door, he clasped her arm and assisted her out of the Jeep. A light breeze blew, carrying the scent of the sea. Only three weeks ago that same water had raged against Hope. The shrieks of the gulls echoed through the air, and the noise of waves washing onto shore soothed her even more. She loved that sound.

As he led her toward his surprise, she asked, "Can I take off the blindfold now? I know we're on a pier."

"But where is the pier?"

"On the Gulf. Not too far from Mom's. It didn't take us long to get here."

"Hope isn't a huge town and traffic was light." Finally, he came to a halt and reached behind her to untie her blindfold.

When the cloth fell away, she faced a twenty-foot sloop, bobbing on the water. "Is this yours?"

He shook his head. "It's Zane's. I learned how to sail when I came here. Zane lets me borrow it when I want to go out on the sea and be truly alone."

"How did it survive the hurricane?"

"Zane took it out of the water."

"Do you sail alone often?"

"I get the hankering about once a month." He hopped down onto the sloop and held his hand out to help her. "My trip is well overdue."

"But if I go, you won't be alone." Stepping down onto the craft, she came up against him as the boat rocked.

He steadied her. "I know, but I thought you could use this time away. I love getting out on the sea, listening to the waves lap against the hull, feeling the sun on my face and the salty breeze powering the sloop to parts unknown. No agenda. Just sailing."

"You've sold me on it. Let's go." She settled herself on the sailboat. "But I've got to warn you, although I grew up on the Gulf, I never learned to sail. I went sailing with friends, but never took lessons. Always too busy doing other things."

"No worries. I've done this many times. This is my gift to you. Enjoy the sun and sea, and don't think about what has to be done when we get back. Okay?"

She smiled as he untied the sloop from the dock. "I like that."

He steered the sloop away from the pier and headed out into the Gulf. "Are you still trusting me?"

"Yeah," she replied slowly, wondering what he was up to.

"I have a destination in mind."

"And you're going to tell me?"

"Nope. You'll figure it out soon enough." He adjusted the mainsail. "I'm curious. What kept you so busy while you were growing up here that you couldn't learn to sail?"

"Two things—dance and cheerleading."

"Neither of which I would have guessed."

"What do you think I did in high school?"

"National Honor Society, Science Club."

"Why?"

"Your mom told me you were valedictorian."

"What else has my mother told you?" She was going to have a word with her mom when she got back home. Every opportunity she got she invited Gideon to come eat with them. On several occasions Kathleen had caught her mother and Gideon laughing over something, but the second she came into the room they would go quiet.

"Just that."

"I did those, too, but my passion was dance."

"Which kind?"

"Ballet."

"Like Swan Lake and the Nutcracker?"

She nodded. "Have you been to a ballet?"

"No, there isn't much opportunity around here."

"True. What did you do in high school?"

"I tried to stay out of trouble."

"No wonder you and Zane are friends. That about describes him."

"I was an angry teen until my last foster parents dragged me to church. At first I sat in the pew determined not to hear anything the pastor was saying." He hitched up one corner of his mouth. "That didn't last long. Once I began listening I realized all that anger at the world was only hurting me. Yeah, I got a raw deal with the death of my parents, but that didn't have to define who I was. So the spring of my junior year, I went out for football."

"You were a jock. That doesn't surprise me."

"Football taught me the importance of being on a team. From there when I graduated from high school, I decided to do something to help others not go through what I did as a child."

"So you became a firefighter."

"It was a kind of therapy for me. I faced what I had feared for years and came out on top."

Had he really? By his own words he kept people at a distance—just like her—afraid to risk getting hurt again.

"What made you become a nurse?"

"Actually, I wanted to be a doctor, but I met Derek and not long after we got married, I became pregnant. My plans changed."

"Why?"

"It didn't seem to fit our future. I loved being

a mother and wanted more children. The cost was too much to do it all so I remained a nurse and gave up my dream of being a doctor. I didn't work much though after Jared came along. Derek wanted me to stay home. He never liked the idea of me working." And she had agreed because she had enjoyed being a full-time mommy, but once her sons started school she'd wanted to go back to work. She and Derek had fought a lot over that. In the end it was easier to volunteer her time than disrupt her family.

"It's not too late."

"Yes, it is. I have a debt to pay off. There's no way I could afford med school."

"Where there is a dream, there is a way."

"Sometimes dreams have to change. Reality has a way of doing that." She shielded her eyes to look out over the glistening water, so tranquil now.

"True. I know that better than some. The day my parents were killed changed my dreams and my reality."

"What was your dream?"

"At eight I wanted to be a firefighter or police officer."

"Then you're living your dream."

"Not exactly. I wanted to grow up to be just like my dad. He was a great father. He wasn't a firefighter, but he was a police officer. My dad would have been so disappointed in me as a teen. I rebelled every chance I got."

With the sails completely up and catching the wind, the boat glided over the smooth water. The shoreline faded the farther out they went. Kathleen relished the beautiful day—the peace, the sense that all was right with the world, that a hurricane hadn't plowed through her hometown.

But on the sloop emotions churned. The past lay exposed between Kathleen and Gideon. She decided to share more of hers. "The disappointment I faced was from my husband. I could never do anything right. I'd made a commitment to him and was determined to make our marriage work, but it was getting so hard. My self-confidence felt attacked from all sides. I questioned everything I did. Then he died and I learned the extent of his betrayal. He kept so many secrets, but right after his funeral they began to come out. By the time the will was read, I realized there was no money, and I most likely would lose the house that meant so much to Derek."

"I'm sorry, Kathleen. That couldn't have been easy."

"The day the bank foreclosed was one of the lowest in my life. I felt a complete failure. My sons were so upset. Their father's death totally changed their lives, and they were groping for stability. That's why I finally decided to come home.

That's what Hope has always meant to me." She gestured toward the distant strip of shoreline. "We're here for seven weeks and a hurricane strikes, totally disrupting Hope. Even moving here hasn't been the stability that Jared and Kip need."

"Maybe you're looking for the wrong kind of stability."

Squinting, she stared at Gideon. "What do you mean?"

"Objects and places don't really offer true stability. They are temporary as we in Hope have found out lately. It's something that happens inside you, a sense of yourself, a peace with yourself." He laughed, little humor in the sound. "Of course, it took Pastor Michael to show me that true stability comes from faith."

Instead of turning away from her faith because of her struggles, should she have turned toward the Lord? Was Gideon right? She did know firsthand how possessions were fleeting. First in Denver and now in Hope, much of what she owned had been taken from her and her sons.

"We're almost to our destination."

Kathleen shifted forward and gazed across the calm sea to an island. She hadn't been paying attention to where they were going, only where they had come from. Much like her life of late. "Which island is this?"

"Dog Island. Zane is one of the owners, and he asked me to check out what the hurricane has done to the place. I told him I would be glad to. He has been turning this island into a refuge for certain species of animals like the different types of eagles. There's a cabin in the heart of the island. He didn't know if it made it or not. He hasn't had time to come out here."

"It sounds like I'm not the only one working too much."

"There is so much to be done rebuilding Hope, and that is what his company does the best. I'm glad he took on Miss Alice's house for cost of supplies. I've heard he's been doing that a lot." Gideon guided the sailboat toward the center of the island to what remained of a pier, a couple of pilings sticking up out of the water.

"The dock is gone."

"Yeah, I was afraid it would be. We can bring this sloop in close. You might roll up your pants and take off your shoes. We'll wade into shore. It shouldn't be too deep."

"Speak for yourself. You're over six feet. I'm only five-two."

"Don't worry. I'll take care of you."

A few minutes later, after Gideon had tied the boat up to the piling nearest shore and thrown an anchor overboard to keep the craft in place, he hopped into the water, holding their shoes and a towel in a bag. "Here, take this." He gave her their belongings. "I'm carrying you to the beach."

She glanced at the water lapping against the bottom of his jean shorts and thought of that foot difference in their heights. "Won't it be hard with your cast?"

"I'll manage." His grin rivaled the sun.

She eased into his arms, conscious of his cast on the left one. He nestled her against him, with the bag clutched to her chest, then waded toward shore but didn't stop until he was up the rise of the beach where the sand was firmer. Then he set her down near a log from an uprooted tree, probably during the hurricane.

"We should wear our shoes. No telling what is hidden in the sand or ground on the island." He sat on the log, leaving her enough room to do the same.

She did, then took her footwear from the bag and passed it to Gideon who used the towel to dry off his wet feet before putting on his deck shoes. After tying her tennis shoes, she glanced up at the area around her. It looked a lot like the beach area in Hope. "I'm not sure this place fared very well."

"At least the island looks like it's intact. Remember the hurricane that split Ship Island into two parts?"

She nodded. "But Fort Massachusetts remained."

"Ready? We'll walk to the cabin before I show you the other side. The waves are a lot bigger on that side. The boys would enjoy swimming here in the summer."

"So you've come out here before. How many times?"

"A few times a year. Sometimes by myself, sometimes there is a group of us to make improvements." He rose, took her hand and tugged her to her feet. "We can't stay too long. I'm just checking to see what will need to be done later."

"I didn't know you and Zane were such good friends."

"We both want to preserve the Barrier Islands and the habitat on them. Most are a part of the park system. This is one that isn't. He didn't want to see it fall into the wrong hands so he got a group together to buy it."

"Zane certainly has changed. Back in high school my best friend's cousin had a crush on him and he hurt her. They dated for a while then he just stopped all of a sudden. He left that summer after she graduated from high school. She didn't know where he went or why. I can still remember listening to her cry in her bedroom."

"People change from when they were teenagers. I certainly have. If I had kept up doing the things I was doing, I would probably be dead by now. I took chances I should never have taken."

She'd changed, too, from having a direction to not having one. From having a dream to living one day at a time with no purpose but to keep her family together, even if it meant losing herself in the process.

"Let's go. Evening will be here soon enough. This will be a whirlwind tour, but I promise I'll bring you and your sons back here to explore the island leisurely, maybe ride the waves."

"Please don't say that to Jared. He'll want to do more than that."

"He's been really good lately. No risks."

"Wait until his cast comes off. I think he has been biding his time."

Gideon waded through the debris and downed tree limbs scattered about the island. "I know that feeling."

"How many more weeks?"

"I go back in four weeks. I've starting doing what Jared does—marking off the days on the calendar."

"But before that there's Thanksgiving and my mother's ambitious plans to celebrate it."

He paused in the path and cupped her face. "She has risen to the occasion as well as you. I'm continually amazed at her ability to organize it. It will be the best Thanksgiving ever."

"Leave it to my mother to find the way to show our thanks and involve hundreds of people."

His warm palm against her cheek rooted her in place. In spite of how the kiss ended the last time, she wanted him to kiss her again, but she would never make the first move. And she didn't have to. Gideon dipped his head toward hers. She dissolved against him, her fingers entwined behind his neck as his mouth settled over hers. For a moment she felt that peace he'd talked about earlier.

Chapter Ten

Next to the lone bell tower at Hope Community Church, Kathleen's mother stretched her arms out wide. "Thank the Lord for this gorgeous day. We have been blessed. This will be the best Thanksgiving ever."

How could her mother say that? There were so many people in need. Kathleen's gaze shifted to the tall pile of boards and debris off to the side of the destroyed newer church. The town had finished the initial trash pickup from the storm and was just starting its second round. It would take more than a few rounds to clean up Hope.

"Why did you want to serve the people here?" Kathleen asked her mother as Gideon pulled up with Jared, Kip and Miss Alice, who had wanted to ride with him.

Sweeping her arm out, she rotated in a full circle. "Look what we have accomplished so far.

Broussard Park is ready for our kickoff of the holiday season tonight. Even the church is coming along. It should be ready for Christmas Eve service in the original church. The Point was one of the hardest hit and after a month, it's beginning to show signs of restoration. That's due to the townspeople."

"You should run for mayor, Mom."

Kip, carrying two sacks of groceries, came to a stop between her and his grandmother. "Mayor? You're running for mayor, Nana? Neat."

"No, please don't say that to anyone. What would I do as mayor?"

"Motivate the town. You're a great organizer. Our current mayor has decided not to run again. In fact, I hear he's thinking of moving away from Hope." Kathleen caught Gideon's gaze as it skimmed down her length, leaving a warm trail where it touched. "What do you think, Gideon. Should my mother run for mayor in the spring?"

"I'd vote for you." He set his paper bags down next to Kip's.

"Me, too." Miss Alice joined them with Jared.

"How did we get from feeding the people who lost their homes to me running for mayor?"

Kathleen shrugged. "But it is still something you should seriously consider."

"Let's get through today first. I think we should set up the tables in the park instead of the church's meeting hall. It's just too pretty to be inside and the park looks great after last week's cleanup. The kids can enjoy the new play equipment."

"Yes, I think we should try it out. Come on, Jared." Kip didn't wait for his little brother. He raced across the park to the new playground.

"Miss Alice, do you need me to bring the rest of your pies?" Jared asked while his gaze strayed to his older brother.

"No, I can manage. You go check out the equipment. We wouldn't want anyone to get hurt if there was a problem."

"Yeah, you're right." Jared gave Miss Alice the two pies he held, then sprinted toward the playground.

Miss Alice laughed. "I didn't have the heart to tell him no. Wait till you see the pie Jared helped me make."

"Should we serve it?" Kathleen remembered her son coming back from Miss Alice's with flour all over him yesterday evening. That had been the first day she'd been back in her mostly repaired house. Zane and Gideon had made it a priority.

"Most definitely. He baked an apple pie and did a great job." Miss Alice winked. "With some assistance from me."

More cars arrived with helpers that her mother had solicited to set up the big Thanksgiving feast she'd planned. Zane stopped to talk with her sons while Pete, his wife and two children joined them with their contribution to the meal—deep fryers for the turkeys. Pete and Gideon went to work setting them up and preparing the birds for the oil. The last of the volunteers—Mildred, a couple of firefighters, her cousin Sally and some of her mother's friends from the ladies group at church appeared with their food and willing hands.

Kathleen's mother asked Gideon to whistle. He put two fingers into his mouth and let out a shrill sound. Everyone turned toward him.

Ruth ascended the steps of the church halfway then turned toward the crowd. "We have three hours to get everything set up. Let's make it special for the folks who have lost most of their possessions."

Kathleen sensed someone approach her from behind and slanted a look at Gideon. The kiss they'd shared last week on Dog Island had haunted her since it occurred. She couldn't seem to get it out of her mind. "Thank you for taking Jared and Kip to the fire station. I wanted to come, but one of the nurses had an emergency and I agreed to fill in for her."

"Did they tell you about the tour?"

"Oh, yes, I heard about it all evening when I got home. Kip's favorite part was the slide. But then I don't know if he enjoyed doing it the most because he truly liked it or because Jared couldn't go down the slide with his cast. Kip made a point of telling me over and over about pretending he was called out to a fire and having to slide down the pole."

"That's okay. I let Jared sound the siren."

"I know. I got dueling stories after that. I went to bed with a headache and those stories running through my mind." But not as much as the kiss she'd received a couple of days before that from Gideon.

"I'm sorry." He circled around in front of her and cut the distance between them. "I didn't mean for you to lose sleep over it."

"I didn't exactly lose sleep over it as much as I had a weird dream with Kip sliding down the pole over and over while Jared sounded the siren continuously. Kip said something about going back again. Are you sure?"

"We have an open house every Christmas. A lot of the kids come and get to play firefighter for a little bit. One year we had to leave because of a fire, and instead of being a disappointment to the children, they were excited to see us in action."

"Kids have a way of turning something around and looking at it from a different view."

"Are you all coming tonight to the Lights On Celebration?"

Kathleen nodded. "We may just stay here until

it gets dark. With the church open, we have all the comforts of home. Zane has been busy."

"Yeah, he's finished the structural restoration of the original church. Now all that is left is the interior makeover."

"Not a small task."

"After church in the meeting room on Sunday, some of us are staying to work on the chapel and classrooms. If you don't have to be at the hospital, why don't you stay and help?"

"Unless an emergency occurs, I should be off."

"Great."

"Hey, you two. We could use some help over here. You can chat later."

Kathleen glanced toward her mother. "The general has spoken. Maybe we should say the mayoral candidate has spoken."

"Do you think she'll run?" Gideon started toward the stacks of tables that Zane had delivered for the people to sit at.

"I hope so. Mom needs a purpose. She was getting too caught up in her soap operas and The Weather Channel. There isn't anyone who knows Hope better than her."

"Everyone needs a purpose."

"Since coming to Hope, I've looked forward to getting up in the morning. The last few years of my marriage, I felt at such a loss, aimlessly going through life."

Gideon hefted one end of a folding table while Kathleen took the other end. "I've been to that place and don't care to go back there."

Kathleen set her part down and flipped the legs out then looked toward Gideon. He stood perfectly still, staring toward the water, his eyebrows slashing downward.

"Gideon?"

When he didn't respond, she said in a louder voice, "Gideon, what's wrong?"

He jerked around, said, "It's Kip. He was by the water and now he isn't. Something's wrong. It doesn't look right," and then began running toward the edge of the Point overlooking the Gulf.

Kathleen heard Gideon and the concern in his voice but for a few seconds the meaning didn't register in her brain. When Gideon was a hundred yards across the park, she raced after him, all the while her heartbeat thundered against her skull.

Gideon reached the edge of the ten-foot cliff, whirled toward her and called out, "Get help. The ground has given way and he's buried under the dirt. There's his ball cap."

Bracing himself with his good arm, he went down the incline. Kathleen hesitated for a breath, wanting to continue toward Kip but instead she hastened back toward the crowd, homing in on Zane and Pete.

"Gideon needs your help. The ground over there—" she wildly waved her hand toward the cliff "—gave way and Kip is buried in the dirt."

Zane was already moving toward his truck before Kathleen had arrived. "I've got some shovels."

Pete and a couple of other firefighters headed across the park toward the water. Kathleen followed. When she reached the men, Pete and their captain clambered down the incline to help Gideon. She started after the pair.

The firefighter left on top stopped her. "Let them take care of it, ma'am. It's a closed-in space and the tide is starting to come in. They need to get him out before that. I've called 911. We'll get him out before they arrive."

She tried pulling away, everything in her screaming for her to be down in the hole created by the ground giving way, but the man clasped her to him. Zane, along with a crowd of people, arrived. He ducked around the firefighter and Kathleen and started down into the hole.

"I need to be there," Kathleen said, watching Zane disappear with the shovels. "Kip needs me."

"They need to get him out first."

The firefighter's calm voice didn't appease the terror building up in Kathleen. The man handed her off to her mother and Sally then corralled everyone back from the edge.

"Get back. The ground has been undermined, probably by the hurricane."

"Mom. Mom. What's wrong with Kip?" Jared clasped her around the waist, fear on his face that matched what she was feeling.

She had to hold it together for both her sons. They would get Kip out, and he would need her then. *Please, Lord, save him.*

Gideon tore at the dirt with both his hands as Pete and his captain joined him. "He's under here and the water's coming in." His tennis shoes sank into the mud at the bottom of the cliff.

As the water rose, the dirt turned to mud, making their digging more difficult. Zane slid down the incline with two shovels and a spade.

Gideon grabbed the smaller tool. "We'd better not use the shovels. We could hit Kip."

"I'll work from the edge inward, carefully." Zane propped one shovel against the bank of dirt behind him while grasping the other one to use.

"I found something!" Pete shouted and scooped up another handful of mud. "A leg."

Gideon and the others concentrated in that area. Kneeling in the water coming in, Gideon estimated where the boy's torso and head would be. Soon he felt Kip's shoulder and increased his speed, working to uncover the child's face while his captain removed the pressure from Kip's chest.

Gideon removed the last layer of muck from around the boy's mouth and nose, then his eyes. Finding his thready pulse at the side of Kip's neck, Gideon released his bottled-up breath. "He's alive." As more of the child was unearthed, Gideon looked up. "Call 911."

"Taken care of!" someone shouted from above.

Wound tight, Kathleen paced in the hallway outside the waiting room. She couldn't sit still while waiting for Kip to come out of surgery. "A collapsed lung, internal injuries. He was standing on the cliff looking out into the water and the next moment he is being swallowed by the ground. Why didn't anyone check the stability of the cliff after the hurricane? Children play in that park. The town is having the Lights On Celebration tonight."

"Not anymore. The mayor has called off the celebration until the park can be checked." Gideon leaned against the wall.

"If you hadn't seen him going over there, he might have disappeared. He could have died before we found him. He could…" She couldn't get the rest of the sentence pass the lump in her throat. She swallowed several times, but it was still too painful to speak.

Gideon pushed himself away from the wall and stepped forward. Drawing her into his embrace, he whispered against the top of her head, "He's all right. They will patch him up and in no time he will be back playing with his friends and Rocky."

"I know the things that can go wrong. What if—"

He pressed his forefinger over her lips. "Have faith he will be all right. Believe it, Kathleen."

"I wish I could. When are things going to stop going wrong?"

He backed up slightly and looked down at her. "Want the truth?"

She nodded. Her throat burned, her stomach roiled.

"Things will never stop going wrong. That's part of life. Problems and complications happen."

"To me," she said. "But why Kip? He's a little boy."

Her mother appeared in the waiting room doorway. "Jared is awake and needs you."

She'd left her younger son on the couch when he'd nodded off a while ago. Before that, he'd been so quiet she'd known he was trying to process what had happened to his big brother. He had rebuked her attempts to talk with him. Now Kathleen hurried to the couch where Jared sat, his shoulders slumped, his hands twisting together. When he lifted his head, a bleakness seized her heart and squeezed.

"Hon, Kip is going to be all right." She had to have faith, as Gideon had said. The alternative was not acceptable.

"He was mad at me for hogging the tire swing. He stomped off. That's why he was at the cliff. He wouldn't have been there—" Her son burst into tears and flung himself into her arms. "I'm sorry. I'm sorry."

"Jared, you did not cause what happened to your brother. It was an accident."

"But it's got to be bad. They're operating on him."

"To fix him up." She placed her finger under his chin and raised it toward her. "He'll be fine. Good as new. You two will be back to arguing in no time."

"Nope. I'll never argue with him again." Tears continued to leak out of Jared's eyes. "Dad had an operation and died a few days later." He clasped himself against her. "What if the same thing happens to Kip?"

His question stole her breath. She gasped for air and tightened her arms around her son. Kathleen closed her eyes, and when she opened them a few seconds later, Gideon stood in front of her, the concern etched into his expression threatening her composure. Jared needed her to be strong, and she didn't feel very strong at the moment.

Gideon knelt and laid his hand on Jared's back. "We can pray for Kip."

Jared's sobs quieted. He pulled back and peered at Gideon. "You think it will help?"

"Yes. God can always help."

Jared shifted toward her. "Mom, can we?"

"Of course, honey. Gideon has an excellent idea."

Gideon reached out and took both Kathleen and Jared's hands, then bowed his head. "Father, we place Kip's care and recovery in Your capable hands. Be with him during this time and surround him with a protective shield. In the name of Jesus Christ. Amen."

The surgeon appeared in the doorway, spied her and crossed the room. "Mrs. Hart, Kip is in recovery. The surgery went well. We were able to stop the internal bleeding, remove his spleen and repair the lung that was punctured."

"Can I see him?" Kathleen rose.

"Yes, you can stay with him in recovery, then we'll move him to his own room."

"Can I see him, too?" Jared hopped up.

"Just your mom right now, but it won't be long before you'll be able to see him," the doctor replied.

Gideon interjected, "While your mom is with Kip, why don't you, me and your grandmother go get something to eat? We didn't get a chance to eat our Thanksgiving feast so let's check out what they have in the hospital cafeteria."

As Kathleen walked toward the exit right behind the doctor, Jared called out, "Promise me you'll come get me the second I can see Kip."

She turned and smiled. "You will be the first one."

"Kathleen, I'll let everyone know about Kip."

"Thanks, Mom."

When she found her son in the recovery room, his eyes closed, his breathing even, she collapsed in a chair near the bed and finally cried. *Thank you, Lord.*

"When can I go home? Rocky has to be missing me." Kip lay in the hospital bed with his IV still in him, his face pale, his eyes dull.

But for a few seconds Kathleen glimpsed a sparkle in his gaze. After five days, Kathleen saw an end to his hospital stay. His chest tube had been removed after the lung re-expanded. He wasn't on as much pain medication from the abdominal surgery and he was complaining. Always a good sign with Kip. "Tomorrow. This will be your last night in here." And mine. She could certainly understand Kip's impatience to be out of the hospital. She'd spent most of her time here with him except when her mother or Gideon relieved her to go home to see Jared and shower.

The door opened, and Jared charged into Kip's room. "I've got more get well cards from your class. After school Amanda gave this one to me and made me promise you'd read it first." He plopped the stack on Kip's bed. "I think she likes you."

"We're friends. That's all."

"What about Ginny? She follows you around on the playground." Jared positioned himself next to Kip as close as he could get.

"Who brought you?" Kathleen asked before her sons got into a fight over girls.

"Gideon."

"Where is he?" She smoothed her hair, hooking it behind her ears.

"I got on the elevator before him and the door closed. He'll be here. He's way too slow."

At that moment Gideon entered the room, carrying a duffel bag that was partially unzipped. A yelp sounded from it.

"What do you have?" As tired as she was, it was so good to see him.

"A surprise." Gideon placed the bag on the empty chair near the bed and lifted Rocky out.

The grin that spread across Kip's face endeared

her even more to Gideon. But still… "Dogs aren't supposed to be in here."

"Shh. Don't tell anyone." Gideon passed the wiggling pet to Kip but kept one hand on the animal. "We can't stay long, but he has been missing you."

Kip buried his face in Rocky's fur. "I've missed him, too."

Jared puffed out his chest. "I didn't say a word about the dog to them."

Gideon ruffled the child's hair. "I appreciate that." He stepped back, allowing Jared to pet Rocky, too.

The dullness in Kip's eyes was replaced with a twinkle. Two patches of red colored his cheeks. The sight of Rocky had done more to lift his spirits than anything else.

"Thanks for doing this, although I should report you to hospital security," Kathleen said.

"I talked with Kip's doctor to make sure it was all right. I'd never do anything to hurt him."

She looked into his gaze. "I know. That's one of the things I like about you." Although Derek had never harmed his sons, those last few years he had been emotionally distant. He stopped doing things with Jared and Kip, and they hadn't understood why. She hadn't either—until she'd discovered her husband's money troubles.

"I gave him a bath so he would be as clean as possible. I figured with Kip coming home tomorrow, Rocky would be all over him then. I didn't think one day would make much difference."

"One day has made a difference. He has been moping around here all day. Even complained there was nothing on TV to watch." She nodded toward the bed where the two brothers were talking civilly and loving on Rocky. Both the boys grinned from ear to ear. "That's a big difference."

"Miss Alice and your mom are planning a small homecoming celebration tomorrow. People have been asking about Kip in the neighborhood. The mayor told Ruth this morning he's waiting to have the Lights On Celebration so Kip can throw the switch on the lights."

"Usually it's a town dignitary. I'll talk with the doctor and find out how restricted Kip's activity will be over the next couple of weeks. So they have reopened the park?"

"Yes and different groups are decorating the whole area. Before it's over with, it's going to look like a Winter Wonderland without the snow. The fire department is taking care of the lighthouse, and we're not sparing anything. It's going to be the best Christmas lighthouse this town has ever seen."

"That's nice," she said while watching Jared

open the cards for Kip to read since her older son was hugging Rocky against his side.

"Nice? It's going to be spectacular. I'm in charge—a desk duty I don't mind."

Kathleen chuckled. "Jared gets his cast off at the end of next week. What about you?"

"The fifteenth of December and I'm counting down the days."

"That evening let me make you that dinner I owe you from way back before the hurricane."

"Sure, I can come to your mom's."

"No, I'm coming to your house. The dinner isn't a family affair."

"Oh, then you've got yourself a date."

"Yes, a date." Ever since that kiss on Dog Island, they had been dancing around each other—friends and yet more.

"That's the best news I've heard all day." Gideon winked then made his way to the bed. "I hate to break up this reunion, but I promised the doc I wouldn't tire you out. Rocky will be waiting for you at your house tomorrow. Jared, can you get Rocky?"

As her son scooped up the dog, Gideon opened the duffel bag. When the animal was inside, he zipped it partway. "I don't want others to get the idea that they can break hospital rules so mum's the word."

Jared paused at the side of his brother's bed,

then suddenly he bent down and gave Kip a hug. "See you tomorrow. I've been taking good care of Rocky for you."

"Is something wrong with Jared?" Kip asked, staring at the door as it closed behind his brother leaving.

"I think he blames himself for what happened to you."

"Why?"

"He said something about a fight you two had over the swing."

"Oh, that. That had nothing to do with the cliff giving way."

"You left the playground and went over to the edge. He thought it was because you were mad at him."

"Not really. I was tired of playing. I like watching the water. One day I'm gonna get myself a boat. I saw one I liked and went over to look at it as it passed by."

"You might say something to Jared about that."

"Why? I think I'll let him suffer a little more. It's kinda nice not arguing all the time."

Kathleen stuck her finger in her ear and wiggled it. "Say that again. I don't think I heard you correctly."

"Oh, Mom. I'm growing up. Fighting is for babies."

"I see. I'll remind you of that when you fight

with Jared again." Because as the sun rose each day, she was sure they would fight again.

The next afternoon, before taking Kip home from the hospital, Kathleen had gone down to the office on the first floor to make arrangements about the bill. With the length of stay and the surgery, even with the insurance she had, her part would be thousands of dollars she didn't have. She still hadn't paid for Jared's broken arm. The woman she'd met with had given her a rough figure—worse than she had thought—but had said not to worry about it just yet until the insurance company settled their part of the bill.

Pulling into her mom's driveway, she switched off the engine and tried to paste a cheerful expression on her face as she turned toward the backseat where Kip was. "Ready? I understand Miss Alice baked you a welcome-home cake. Your favorite—chocolate fudge."

"Really. How did she know? Nana?"

"Yep. There are a few people here to see you, but the second you're tired let me know. I'll clear them out. I don't want you overdoing it."

"Mooom, quit babying me. I'm almost ten."

She climbed from her car and opened the back door. "I've got news for you. I'll always be concerned about you even when you are a grown-up and living on your own."

Jared slammed open the front door and ran down the steps, barely managing to stop before barreling Kip over. "You're home. I'm starved, and Nana said I can't have any cake until you're here."

Kip rolled his eyes. "You'll survive."

"C'mon. You get the first slice. Miss Alice said so." Jared pulled on Kip's arm.

"Jared Taylor Hart, let go of your brother's arm. He will be inside in a second. How about you come over here and help me take our stuff inside." Kathleen swung the small suitcase out of the back and handed it to Jared, then faced the house. "When did you all put up the Christmas decorations?"

"Yesterday afternoon. Gideon helped me and Nana. We've got the tree up but no decorations on it yet. We were waiting for you to come home. Maybe we can do that later today."

"Slow down, Jared." Kathleen grabbed the sack of items she'd been given at the hospital for Kip. "I doubt we will tonight. Maybe tomorrow."

"Do you know Miss Alice doesn't put up any decorations? She told me it was too much effort for just her." Jared walked ahead of her and Kip toward the porch, jabbering and not caring they weren't keeping up.

At the front door, he finally stopped and waited for them. "So what do you think?"

Kip scrunched his forehead. "What about?"

"Decorating Miss Alice's house for her. Our gift to her. Wanna help me?"

"Before you go planning your brother's life, I think you need to realize he will be restricted for the next several weeks while he continues to heal. He won't be able to do a lot of what he used to. Recovery from surgery takes time."

"Sure, Mom." Jared opened the screen door then the main one. "But he can help me with Miss Alice. That shouldn't be a lot of work."

When Kathleen, Kip and Jared entered the living room, she came to a halt, taking in the sea of people crowded into the small area. This was not her definition of a small celebration.

Gideon moved to her side. "Glad you're here. I didn't know what we were going to do with Jared."

"We need to use the same dictionary. In mine, this wouldn't be defined as small."

"Well, it started out that way, just a few friends and family. Then the firefighters who helped rescue Kip wanted to come. After that, one neighbor after another asked if they could drop by and see how he was doing. They all dropped by at the same time."

Stunned, Kip scanned the people in front of him, his gaze pausing on several of his classmates, especially a pretty young girl with long brown hair and blue eyes. Amanda? Ginny? Kathleen peered at her son. His cheeks reddened, and he looked down at the floor by his feet.

She turned and whispered into Gideon's ear. "It looks like my son doesn't care who is here so long as that pretty brunette is."

"Ah, Amanda, the one who decorated his card with glitter and hearts."

"I thought that might be her."

Her mother climbed up on the coffee table, nodding to Gideon. He gave a loud whistle and the room quieted, except for a few whispers and giggles. "Mayor Thomas has a few words to say before we cut the cakes."

Kathleen leaned toward Gideon again, taking in a whiff of his lime aftershave lotion. She immediately thought of her favorite pie—key lime. "I thought there was only one."

"When your mother saw all the people showing up, she had me go buy a couple more, along with some drinks and ice cream."

"You'd think this was a birthday party."

"The ice cream was Jared's idea. He went with me. Guess what kind I have."

"Vanilla."

"Yep. I tried to talk him into chocolate, but he told me he didn't like chocolate. What kid doesn't?"

"My son. He's never been a big fan of it. But

give him a bowl of ice cream, so long as it isn't chocolate, and it will be gone in no time. Takes after his mother."

"What flavor do you like?"

"Cookie dough. I never got many cookies baked because I ate half of the dough. Got sick a couple of times when I ate too much. My mother didn't take pity on me. How about you?"

"Chocolate. I do like chocolate in any form."

One side of his mouth quirked into a grin that flipped her stomach. He was totally focused on her, and her knees went weak. She gripped his arm to steady herself. "Sorry. I haven't slept much the past week. You know it isn't easy sleeping in a hospital unless they knock you out. Too much noise and people."

"Yeah, you would have thought you had that figured out since you work in one."

"Didn't think about it until I had to stay five nights. When my husband was in the hospital, he didn't want me to, and I needed to be home with the kids."

The mayor made his way to the sturdy coffee table and joined her mother. "This is a great time for me to ask Ruth if she will run for my office. Don't y'all think she should?"

Her mother blushed beet red. "When you said you had a few words to share with the crowd, I didn't think it was about me running."

"I've been hearing rumors and I thought it was time I tried to talk you into running for mayor."

Everyone cheered, Kip and Jared the loudest with Gideon whistling.

"See. They all want you to be our next mayor."

"I have no experience."

"Have you lived in Hope all your life?" the mayor asked her mother.

She nodded.

"You know everything about Hope and probably just about everyone in town. C'mon, let's hear it for Ruth as our next mayor."

Ruth raised her hands to calm the roar of approval. "Why don't you run again?"

"Because I've been mayor for eight years, and it's my time to step down. I'm retiring."

"I've already retired from one job. I don't need a second one."

"You might not, but the town needs someone who cares. That's you, Ruth. Look at the Thanksgiving feast you organized."

"We had to postpone it because of the accident."

"Just the celebration part. The food was distributed to the people who needed it." Mayor Robert Thomas took her mother's hand. "We've been friends for a long time. Since elementary school.

You're what this town needs now. Promise me you'll think about it."

"I—I—" Her mother stared down at their clasped hands. "I don't know what to say."

"All I'm asking is you think about it." The mayor's face lit up like a Christmas tree.

"He knows he's got my mom," Kathleen whispered to Gideon in the silence that enveloped the room. She lowered her voice even more and bent close to Gideon, saying, "I heard that once they were an item before my dad came on the scene. You would think he had proposed to Mom in front of the neighborhood the way she is acting."

Gideon laughed, breaking the quiet. Suddenly, the room was filled with chatter and cheers.

Her mother extracted her hand from the mayor's and stepped down from the table.

Robert Thomas raised his arms and signaled for silence. "My other reason for being here is to welcome Kip Hart home from the hospital. His accident only reinforces how cautious we need to be. We're still discovering all the effects of the hurricane on Hope. We don't want any more children hurt."

Jared took Kip's arm and tugged him through the crowd toward the dining room. "I don't know about you guys, but I'm starved. Time for cake and ice cream."

A sprinkle of laughter rippled through the group, neighbors parting to allow Jared and Kip through.

"They know it's dangerous to get in the way of a child and cake and ice cream." Practically plastered against Gideon, Kathleen moved away from him. She released a long, slow breath. "I'd better go rescue Miss Alice and Mom."

"Those ladies don't need rescuing." He grasped her hand and drew her toward the front door. "You need to rest."

Before she could say anything, Gideon had her on the porch and sitting in a white wicker chair. "What just happened?"

"I'm rescuing *you*. You're tired. The past week has worn you down."

She cupped her face. "I look that bad?"

"No, but I can tell something is wrong. Did the doctor say something today?"

She shook her head, wishing that she didn't always have a hard time hiding her feelings. "Kip will be fine in time. By Christmas he'll probably be chasing Jared around the house."

"Then what is it?"

"Quit being so perceptive."

"I haven't been accused of that before."

"It's really nothing. There is just so much to do. I can't believe Christmas is weeks away. I started thinking of all I need to do, and I got tired."

He scrutinized her for a long moment, his eyes boring into her as if he were trying to read her thoughts.

She stiffened, determined not to squirm under his probing.

"As you know, I have a fairly normal schedule until after I see the doctor on December 15th, so what can I do to help you?"

"You've already done enough."

"That's not the point. The point is you need help. How can I help you?"

Don't press me about what's wrong. She couldn't tell him she was even more in debt than before in spite of having health insurance. Twenty percent of thousands was still a lot of money—money she didn't have. She would have to figure out something when she wasn't so exhausted.

She had to say something to Gideon. The expectant look on his face told her he wouldn't let it go until she did. "You could come tonight and help us decorate the tree. I don't think Jared will rest until the tree is fully up. We usually do it Thanksgiving weekend. One of our long-standing traditions."

"That's all?"

"Well, it's a start. If I can think of anything else, I'll be sure to say something. Truthfully, you being here is nice."

"Nice?" His smile grew. "I guess that is better than okay."

His infectious grin spread through her. "That's all you're gonna get. We'd better get back inside. I want some of that ice cream. I know where my mom's stash of caramel sauce is. That goes great with vanilla ice cream." As she pushed to her feet, she prayed that Gideon dropped the subject of what was wrong. Her problems were hers—not his.

Chapter Eleven

"Mom, where's the hot chocolate?" Kip sat on the couch putting hooks on the ornaments.

"Hot chocolate? You want that? It's fifty-eight degrees outside." Kathleen took another Christmas ball from her son and found a space on the eight-foot artificial tree.

"Yeah, it's a tradition. We've done it *forever*."

"That was in Denver where it's cold."

"Please."

"I don't have the ingredients for hot chocolate." Her mother handed a homemade decoration, one Kathleen had made in grade school, to Jared to place near the top of the tree.

He climbed the stepladder and reached up to hang the ornament on the fake pine. "You can go get some. I'm with Kip. We can't decorate the tree without hot chocolate."

Kathleen peered at the nearly finished work of

chaos standing in front of the picture window in the living room.

"I'll go get it. What do you need?" Gideon asked.

"Tell you what. We'll take a break. You need to rest, Kip. Gideon and I will go to the store and get the ingredients. Then after we've had our hot chocolate, we'll finish the tree."

"I'm on a roll. I don't need to rest." Jared hooked another ball on the same limb as two others. The artificial limb drooped.

Ruth sat in a chair near the tree. "Tell you what, Jared. Why don't you go see if Miss Alice would like to share some hot chocolate and leftover cake with us?"

Kip laid his head on a sofa pillow and closed his eyes. "Hurry back."

Jared went out the front door with Gideon and Kathleen and raced across the lawn to Miss Alice's.

"Let's take my car. It's right here." Kathleen dug into her purse and retrieved her keys, then tossed them to Gideon. "I'll even let you drive."

When he tried to start the vehicle, a loud cranking sound echoed through the interior, grating on her already frazzled nerves. She held her breath when he attempted it a second time. Dead. Now what?

"I don't think it's going to turn over this time." Still, Gideon turned the key in the ignition again.

She heard nothing but the choking noise of a dying car. She didn't have any extra money—not for Christmas, not for the hospital and certainly not for car repairs.

"Let me get my Jeep and use that. Pete knows about cars, and I'll have him come over and take a look. It could be something simple he can fix." He opened the door. With the interior light shining in the darkness, he angled toward her. "Don't worry about it tonight. We'll make hot chocolate and sit around and pretend we are in front of a fire."

Tears tightened her throat. *Don't cry. Don't ruin this evening.* It wouldn't change the fact that the car would need an infusion of cash to get running.

Gideon sat there, his gaze fixed on her. "Are you okay?"

Her emotions screamed for release. She wanted to rile, to yell, to cry. "Fine," she said. Averting her face, she fumbled with the handle to open her door.

His hand on her shoulder compelled her to shift toward him. "I thought so earlier. Something is wrong. Sometimes talking about it helps."

"No, it won't. I'm tired. That's all. Don't make it out to be something it isn't. Lately a few things have gone wrong. Haven't you had one thing too many happen to you and you just want to give up?"

"Sure, but Kip is on the mend and the town will recover."

Tears crowded her eyes. Why couldn't her body do what she wanted? Frustrated, she balled her hands, fingernails digging into her palms. "I'll be much better tomorrow after a good night sleeping in my own bed. Hospital cots aren't the best place to sleep." She hurriedly thrust open the passenger door and exited before he asked any more probing questions. The money was her problem, and she'd never been comfortable sharing her problems with others. She'd learned in her marriage to keep them to herself.

Standing back in the dining room doorway, Gideon finished the last sip of his delicious second cup of hot chocolate, watching the last of the decorations being put on the tree by Kip, Kathleen, Jared and Ruth.

"I declare that is the most unusual Christmas tree I've seen in a long time. There is a pine tree under all those ornaments, isn't there?" Miss Alice staked her claim on the chair with the stool in the living room.

"Somewhere under there," Ruth said with a laugh, moving back to get a good look at the overall picture. "We do have a lot of decorations, an accumulation of many years of collecting Christmas memories."

"Jared, you might go a little to the left then reach up a few inches. There's one blank space left without anything on it." Miss Alice pointed toward an area on the tree.

"Oh, yeah, I see. Thanks." On the stepladder, Jared glanced over his shoulder at Miss Alice at the same time he leaned to the side.

The child wobbled. Jared flapped his arms to get his balance. The sequined ball went flying across the room as he finally grabbed hold of the nearest object—the Christmas pine—to steady himself on the ladder. But instead, he kept plunging downward to the floor with the tree tumbling with him.

Gideon shot forward but all he caught was air. He looked down. Jared lay in the middle of a mountain of ornaments, some broken, with some green pine poking out. The look of confusion on the child's face evolved into horror as he took in what happened. His eyes became round like perfectly drawn circles.

There was nothing but complete silence for a few seconds until Jared struggled to get up and crushed several more decorations under him. Gideon offered the child his hand, which he took.

Gideon lifted him free of the mess and set him a couple of feet away.

Jared opened his mouth to speak. Nothing came out. He snapped it closed.

Finally, Ruth began laughing. "Well, that is one way to weed out some of the ornaments."

Kip chuckled, followed by Miss Alice.

Gideon's attention riveted to Kathleen, who stood frozen, shock on her face.

"Are you all right, Jared?" she finally asked, a taut thread woven through her words.

The child nodded.

Kathleen's stunned expression melted into relief, and she sagged back against the windowsill.

"I think we can salvage this." Gideon stooped and grasped the trunk then hoisted the tree to an upright position.

Some of the loose ornaments fell to the floor, a couple shattered among the shards of other broken ones. Gideon made sure the pine was stable, and then he backed away. "In answer to your earlier question, Miss Alice, there is a tree underneath there."

Kathleen shoved herself from the window ledge. "More hot chocolate anyone?"

Everyone quickly said yes.

"I'll help you get it." Gideon quickly trailed

Kathleen into the kitchen while the others discussed how to clean up the mess.

Kathleen covered the distance to the stove where a pan of hot chocolate was still on a burner. "Poor Jared. He's going to be so upset with himself." She slanted a look at Gideon. "Mom really did have too many ornaments, but she never would get rid of any of them. She has been collecting them from before I was born. She always insisted the boys make her something for the tree as her present every year."

A memory invaded his thoughts. The boxes of Christmas decorations stored in his childhood home in the attic. All burned up—gone forever. After that he hadn't collected many—only a handful given to him by friends over the years. The small two-foot tree he put up at Christmas had a lot of bare places on it.

As Kathleen poured the drink into the mugs, he came to her side, inches from her. The sound of laughter drifted from the living room. He smiled. "This could have been a disaster."

"Next year all those bare places on the tree now will be filled with new decorations. It was an accident. The topping on a difficult day. I figure I need to cut my losses and go to bed."

"That might not be a bad idea. I'll help your mother clean up the mess. Go on. You're right. This past week has been hard on you."

"But what about the ornaments that have to be put back on the tree?"

"We'll take care of it." He captured her hands and turned her toward him. "Go. Rest. You deserve it."

"But this is my…"

"What?"

"My family. I can't ask you to fill in for me."

"You aren't asking me. I'm volunteering. No, I'm insisting." He cupped her chin and lifted her head so he could look into her eyes. He grazed his forefinger across the top of her cheek. "I see it there. You're exhausted."

"I can't let you do my job. This is my family."

"Why not let me? I'll borrow yours for the rest of the evening. Tomorrow you'll be better rested."

"You know when I agreed to decorating the tree tonight, I'd forgotten how much work it could be, especially a second time."

"I saw that when all you did was sink down on the windowsill and stare at your son when he fell."

"Yeah, I didn't have the energy to react. He has his share of accidents, but this was a doozy. I'm glad Mom took it so well."

"Ruth goes with the flow."

"That's something I'm still learning from her," she said in a voice that reflected the world crashing down on her.

He brushed his lips across hers, then urged her toward the door into the hallway. "C'mon. Off to bed with you." He watched her walk toward the stairs, her shoulders slumped, her step slow.

She bent over the banister to look at him. "Thank you."

"You're welcome."

As she disappeared from his view, he remembered bits and pieces of their interaction throughout the day. Something was wrong. Kip's accident had been traumatic, but there was something else going on with Kathleen. He'd given her several opportunities to confide in him, but she hadn't. Frustration churned his gut. He was falling for her, and she was putting up barriers between them. He needed to shore up his own walls, protect himself, but he was afraid he was too late.

"Kip wanted to know where the hot chocolate—" With glitter sparkling in the light on his jeans and shirt, Jared paused in the entrance from the dining room and panned the kitchen. "Where's Mom?"

"It was past her bedtime."

"She doesn't have one."

Gideon crossed to the tray with the full mugs and picked it up. "She was tired, and I told her I would make sure everything was cleaned up from your little disaster."

Jared yawned. "You know, I'm tired, too. I think I'll go to bed—after my hot chocolate."

"Sorry, I'm not buying it." Another yawn made Gideon chuckle. "Still not. You're stuck on cleanup duty."

A grin spread over his face. "Oh, well, at least I get to stay up past my bedtime."

"When is it?"

Jared leaned to the side and peered at the clock on the wall behind Gideon. "In ten minutes."

"Guess you're gonna miss it."

"Yes." Jared pumped his arm in the air.

Gideon carried the tray into the living room and passed the mugs around to everyone, except the one who requested the hot chocolate. Kip lay on the couch asleep.

"Should I wake him?" Gideon set the tray with the last mug on the coffee table in front of the couch.

"Young man, don't you know you never wake a sleeping child? Wait, maybe that's a sleeping baby." Miss Alice sipped her drink.

"Where's Kathleen?" Ruth put the lid on an empty ornament box then sat with her hot chocolate cupped between her hands.

"She went to bed." Gideon looked back at Kip. "I can take him up to his room."

"That would be great if you think you can with your cast." Ruth took a swallow from her cup.

"Sure." He thought about the time he'd carried Kathleen to the beach on Dog Island. He'd enjoyed the feel of her in his arms.

Squatting by the couch, Gideon carefully scooped up Kip and rose. The boy snuggled against Gideon and draped one arm over his shoulder. His eyes closed, Kip murmured something Gideon couldn't understand and settled against him.

A few minutes later, he laid the boy on his bed and covered him with a blanket. He stared down at the child and wondered what it would feel like being a father. When Kip had fallen last week, his heart had plummeted and a gripping fear had taken over as he'd never experienced. He'd rescued children before, but that had been different.

When he returned to the living room, Miss Alice sat forward, then stood. "I'd better be going."

"Let me walk you home." Gideon started for the foyer and opened the front door.

"Good night, y'all. Thanks for sharing this with me. It's been years since I've participated in decorating a tree." Miss Alice shuffled toward Gideon, a softness in her expression that a month ago hadn't been there.

He offered her his arm, and they descended the porch steps.

"Those boys are good kids, but they need a

father." Miss Alice's declaration broke the silence between them halfway up her sidewalk to her house. "If you're not interested, maybe one of your friends. That Zane fellow is nice. I like him. He did a good job fixing my house."

"I don't think Zane is looking for a wife."

"Are you?"

He nearly faltered on the stairs leading to the porch, quickly grabbing hold of the railing. "I hadn't really thought about it."

"You'd better stake your claim fast. She needs a good man to take care of her."

"Why do you say that?" Gideon stopped at the front door, shifting from foot to foot.

"She's sad. I see it in her eyes. From what Ruth has told me and what I see, I don't think her path has been easy."

"What has Ruth told you?"

Alice dug into the pocket of her sweater and pulled out her key, then inserted it into the lock. "That, young man, is something you will have to ask Ruth or Kathleen. I don't gossip. Well, occasionally I have but not in this case."

"Good night, Miss Alice." He turned to leave.

He descended the steps when Miss Alice said, "Don't end up like me—alone all your life. It isn't all it's cut up to be."

He glanced back at the woman, but she went

into her house and shut her door. As he walked back to Ruth's, darkness surrounded him with a hint of a chill in the air. Could he risk his heart with Kathleen? Miss Alice's words about being alone pricked his heart, threatening his belief that he was better off not caring too much for others and going through life more an observer than a participant. This past month he hadn't been. Was it because of the hurricane or Kathleen that he'd gotten more involved than he usually did?

When he reentered Ruth's house, he found Jared and her in the living room with broom and dustpan, cleaning up the pieces of broken decorations. "I thought if I stayed gone long enough you two would have this all taken care of."

Jared giggled. "I should have asked to take Miss Alice home." He moved the dustpan away, tilting it forward enough that its contents spilled all over the floor again.

"Jared, pay attention." Ruth's loud sigh conveyed her annoyance.

Gideon bridged the distance between them and took the broom from Ruth. "I'll help Jared in here."

She gave him a grateful look. "Then I'll take care of cleaning up the dishes we used." After gathering the tray and mugs, she strolled toward the kitchen.

"I didn't mean to dump the pieces." Jared's mouth drooped in a pout. "I don't mean to cause trouble."

"I know. Sometimes it just happens. Here, hold the pan while I sweep it up again." As he worked, he saw Jared's sagging shoulders and tight mouth. "What happened tonight reminded me of a time when I was eight and couldn't wait until Christmas Day to open all the presents under the tree. My parents were getting ready in their bedroom to go out. I decided to sneak a peek when they weren't in the room. I wheedled my way under the tree, wanting to get my hands on the big box in the back. I wiggled the wrong way and the tree came down on top of me."

"You did? What did your parents do?"

The memory was seared into his mind as though it had happened yesterday. "They heard the noise and came running. When they found me, they must have laughed for five minutes before they got the tree off me. I didn't understand why they weren't mad at me. It had taken us hours to decorate the tree, and I had destroyed it in seconds."

"They didn't do anything to you?"

"Oh, they did. I had to clean it up all by myself and put everything back on the tree without their help. They decided not to go out that evening and instead sat there on the couch watching me, talking to each other and ignoring my whining." He wouldn't trade that memory for anything. It made his parents seem so real to him for a few minutes.

"Where are your parents?"

"They died years ago."

"My dad did. I miss him every day."

"I miss my parents every day."

"Everything is so different now."

"How so?"

"Mom has to work a lot. She's always worrying. Nana told me worrying only makes the problem worse."

Grinning, Gideon finished sweeping the last pieces into the pan. "She's right. But it doesn't stop me from worrying."

"Why doesn't it?" Jared kept his gaze fastened onto the pan as he lifted it and walked slowly to the trash can, then dumped the contents into it.

"I've never really found that worrying about a problem solves it. It just makes me stressed over it, but for so long it has been a habit of mine I'm trying to change."

Jared cocked his head to the side. "Yeah, you're right. I worried about Kip when he was in the hospital. But that didn't really make him get better. I think my prayers helped. Nana and me prayed every night he was there."

"That's great. You're a good brother."

Jared puffed out his chest. "Yeah, I am."

Ruth reappeared in the living room. "This looks nice. You wouldn't know you toppled the tree."

"Except there aren't as many ornaments on it. Maybe Kip and me can make some to put on it this weekend."

"I'd like that." Ruth hugged her grandson.

"How about you, Gideon? Will you help us on Saturday?"

"Sure. I can't think of a nicer way to spend the day." As he said those words, he realized he had meant every one of them. When he had kidded Kathleen about borrowing her family for the night, he hadn't realized how it would affect him. He wanted a family for himself.

Kathleen sat at the kitchen table gluing sequins on a plain gold ornament while Jared and Kip glued paper rings together to make a garland for Miss Alice.

"Did ya get it?" Jared asked the second Gideon came into the room on Saturday.

"No *how are you?*" Gideon bent down and rubbed Rocky behind his ears.

"Hi. They've been wondering what was taking you so long. They wanted me to take them to the store to find you," Kathleen said with a chuckle. "I had to remind them my car is being fixed and they would have to walk. They decided to wait a little longer."

"Miss Alice is gonna be so surprised." Kip used the scissors to cut some more red and green strips of construction paper.

"How big is the tree?" Jared dabbed some glue on the end of the ring to hold it together.

"I got a live tree in a pot. It's about three feet high. Then if she wants me to, I'll plant the pine after Christmas."

"To replace the tree she lost. I like that." Kip paused and leaned down to pay attention to Rocky sitting by his chair.

"Where's Ruth? I thought she would be in the middle of this."

"She's getting ready to leave. We decided Nana should take Miss Alice out shopping while we decorate her house. That was my idea." Jared patted his chest.

Gideon took the chair next to Kathleen across from the boys. "How are we going to get into Miss Alice's house?"

"She gave Mom a spare key when she moved back into her house. I guess with everything that has happened, she has decided that might be for the best rather than us breaking down her door if we think she's in trouble." She'd missed Gideon the past few days, working at the hospital as much as possible to make up for taking off while Kip was there.

"How long do you think we'll have?" Gideon scooted his chair closer to the table, his arm brushing against Kathleen.

"An hour, probably, so we need to be finished with these decorations when Mom leaves."

"We're almost done. Look at this." Jared, with Kip's help, held up the long paper garland for Miss Alice's tree.

"That ought to go around all of it." She slanted a glance toward Gideon who made a design with glue then sprinkled red glitter on the plain gold ornament. "What time are we going to the Lights On Celebration at the Point?"

"Six. With Kip throwing the switch we want a good place to see it. Wait until you see what the fire department did with the lighthouse. We went all out this year. Y'all might want to bring your sunglasses."

"At night?" Jared wrinkled his nose.

"You'll see what I mean in a few hours."

"The hospital did the Christmas tree." Kathleen began gathering the decorations in a box to take to Miss Alice. "I helped some yesterday afternoon after work."

"I wanted to come, but Mom wouldn't let me. She said I needed to rest. That's all I've been doing. I'm getting bored with watching TV and sleeping." Kip put the last ring on the garland.

"I don't want you to overdo it."

Purse in hand, Ruth stopped in the entrance into the kitchen. "I'm going to get Miss Alice. Give me ten minutes then go on over. We won't be gone more than an hour. She wants to rest before tonight's celebration."

After her mother left, Kathleen placed the paper garland on top of the ornaments. "Let's clean this up. We won't have a lot of time when we come back here before dinner."

"Mom, I think someone needs to keep a look out for Nana and Miss Alice leaving. I'll do it." Jared hopped up from his chair and raced toward the living room.

Kathleen opened her mouth to tell him it wasn't necessary, but he'd fled so fast she'd barely formed the first word in her mind. "I've got to harness some of his energy. I could use it."

"I'd better help him." Kip followed his little brother from the room although at a much slower pace.

"We're alone at last." Gideon waggled his eyebrows. "I thought they would never leave."

Kathleen laughed. "And what did you have in mind?"

He bent toward her and kissed her quick on the

mouth. "That. I'd been thinking about it since I first came in here." He started to pull away.

Kathleen stopped him with a hand on his arm. "Hmm. I don't call that a kiss. Maybe a peck, but certainly not a kiss."

He locked his gaze on her lips. "You're mighty picky today. What is a kiss in your book?"

She smiled, one that came from the depths of her heart, and wound her arms around his neck, tugging him toward her. Her mouth connected with his, and she poured everything into it until she forgot to breathe and finally had to step back to take a deep gulp of air.

"Ah, I see what you mean. We might need to practice some more later." He moved back quickly as the sound of footsteps neared the kitchen. "When we're alone again," he added in a whisper as Jared and Kip burst into the room.

"They're gone," both boys said at the same time.

"Let me get the key. Jared and Kip, carry one of the boxes of decorations. I'll bring the large Christmas card you two made for her." Kathleen crossed to the desk and pulled out the drawer where Miss Alice's house key was.

Jared examined the kitchen table. "You two didn't do a good job of cleaning up. The glitter is everywhere, paper on the floor. What were you all doing?"

Kathleen wasted no time coming up with an excuse. "I decided to leave some for you and Kip while we wait for the pizzas to be delivered."

Kip punched Jared in the arm. "Why did you go and say that? When are you gonna ever learn to keep your mouth shut?"

"I was just wondering." Jared stuck his tongue out and hastened from the room with his box.

When Kip went after his little brother, Gideon blew out a breath of air. "Quick thinking."

"If we aren't one step ahead of our kids, we get trampled. Not fun in the least."

Gideon grabbed the pot with the small pine. "Sounds like you've been trampled a few times."

"I wish it were only a few. I lost count way back."

An hour later the four of them finished with Miss Alice's living room, confining their holiday decorating to that one room she spent most of her time in. On the front door the boys hung their three-foot-by-two-foot card with the outside displaying a huge fir dripping with ornaments and lights and packages beneath it.

With Kip on one side and Jared on the other, Kathleen stood in the middle of the living room. Voices from the front porch announced her mother and Miss Alice's approach.

"We should hide like a surprise birthday party." Jared scanned the area. "I can, behind that chair."

He started for his hiding place, but Kathleen grasped his shirttail and halted his movement. "I think she'll know something is up with that huge card on her door. Besides, we don't want to give her a heart attack."

Cottonballs whined and weaved in and out of their legs as the knob on the front door turned.

"Let me put this sack down and get my reading glasses on. Who would leave me such a big card?" Miss Alice moved into the foyer and caught sight of them in the entrance to the living room. She gasped, dropping her sack and splaying her hand over her heart. "Oh, my, what are y'all doing here? Y'all scared the—" Then she took several more steps until she saw all the decorations. Her mouth fell open.

While Miss Alice remained rooted to the floor, Jared came up to her and pulled on her arm. "Something's leaking all over the tiles."

Miss Alice blinked and swept around, her hand covering her mouth. "My eggs. They're broken."

Kathleen skirted around the woman and stooped to clean up the mess. "I'm sorry. I'll replace them. We wanted to show you how much we care about you and give you a little bit of Christmas." Gathering up the egg carton, she placed it into the torn sack while taking out the other grocery items. Thankfully, none of them were broken.

A suspiciously shiny sheen to her eyes, Miss Alice surveyed the living room, saying, "Don't worry about the eggs. I can't believe y'all did this for me. No one has done…" Her voice cracked, and she lowered her head, pulling a tissue from her coat pocket and dabbing at her face.

"It was my idea," Jared piped in.

Kip stepped forward. "No, it wasn't. I thought of it and talked to you about it. I came up with the big card on the door."

"No, you didn't." Jared sent his brother a glare.

"Boys, that's enough. Let's say this was a co-operative idea between Jared and Kip." Kathleen walked toward the kitchen. "I'm throwing these away. I don't want to come back in here and see you two fighting."

She strode to the trash can and dumped in the sack and carton of eggs, straining to hear what was going on in the living room. All she heard were murmurs. She rushed back to find Miss Alice seated in her recliner, tears streaking down her face.

"I'd forgotten what Christmas was about until this year. You couldn't have given this old lady a better gift."

"We made everything in here." Kip beamed.

"Well, except the tree. But everything else." Jared stood next to his brother, his grin as big as Kip's.

"I'll never forget this. And you two can play soccer in my front yard anytime you want." Miss Alice swiped the tissue across each eye, then stuffed it back into her pocket.

While Kip brought Miss Alice the Christmas card from the front door so she could read the inside, Kathleen watched their neighbor interact with her two sons. A warmth flowed through her. Her sons still bickered, but for this project they had worked side by side with little fighting. In the past week they hadn't said once they wished they were in Denver. Hope was becoming their home. At least one thing was working out as she'd prayed. If only the rest of it would.

At the front of the crowd at Broussard Park in a semicircle around the lighthouse, Kathleen huddled in her light jacket, not having expected the wind to be as cold as it was, blowing off the water. She hugged herself and tried to focus on what Mayor Thomas was saying.

Next to her, Gideon drew her close to him, wrapping his arms around her. His warmth spread through her, alleviating the chill some. She cherished the feel of his embrace, the sense of being protected from the elements. "The temperature is dropping. A front must be moving through. It's always a little cooler here, which is great in the summer."

She turned her head and whispered, "Some people came better prepared than I did. I'm looking forward to a cup of hot chocolate."

Gideon's face, only inches from hers, threw her heartbeat into a fast tempo. The cold fled completely as the mayor finished his little speech about the future of Hope.

"It's time to turn on the lights. A beacon of hope in the dark. Ships passing by will be able to see our little light display. Hope may have been hit six weeks ago, but we aren't down. There will be a new Hope rising even better than before. Kip Hart will flip the switch this year on our Lights On Celebration. Kip, are you ready?"

Nodding, her son positioned himself next to a big red button.

"Okay. Ten. Nine," the mayor said with everyone as usual joining in the countdown. "Eight. Seven. Six. Five. Four. Three. Two. One."

Kip pressed the button and bright lights flooded the park—thousands and thousands of them, glittering and dazzling.

But Kathleen's gaze fastened onto the lighthouse the fire department had decorated. Red, white and blue lights covered the whole surface of the white structure as though the building was wrapped in an American flag. "Stunning."

"I'm glad you like it. It was my idea. A tribute to our soldiers and citizens who continually fight to make this country better. All I have to do is look around at the people in this crowd."

The warmth of his breath tickled her neck. She shivered.

"Still cold?"

The crowd began to clap at the display not only on the lighthouse, but on the ten-foot Christmas tree standing tall at the edge of the cliff as if it defied the sea to take it down as it had so many others in the hurricane. The park's pines, live oaks, stripped of their Spanish moss, and magnolia trees left from the storm were lit up in white like stars glinting in the night sky.

Kip made his way through the people surrounding the mayor. "Mom, what did ya think?"

"You did great."

"The mayor told me they found a few more areas along the cliff that had to be shored up. That I prevented others from being hurt. I helped save some people."

She was glad some good had come out of the tragedy, but it didn't make it any less painful.

"I'm hungry. Can I go get some dessert and hot chocolate?" Jared wedged himself in front of Kathleen.

"I was thinking that very thing." The church would block a lot of the chilly wind. A much better place to enjoy the treats her mother's ladies' group had fixed. "If we hurry, we can be first in line."

Jared shot forward, nearly knocking into a young woman in his haste. Kip trailed his brother at a more sedate pace, still not up to his usual active level.

"I probably shouldn't have said that. But then with everyone who turned out for the celebration, it would be nice to be at the front of the line."

Gideon glanced around. "I think others have the same idea."

"At least we'll be out of the wind."

Gideon waved at Pete and his wife. "We could break in line."

"You're such a rebel."

"Your mom said something about making divinity."

"She makes the best in town. Probably the state. I don't know how I'm going to carry on her tradition. Mine isn't nearly as good."

"Y'all have a lot of traditions at Christmas."

"Yeah, passed down from my grandmother. There is a comfort to them. Kip and Jared will feel right at home here because we've done the same thing since they were born. We were a little late with the tree because of the accident, but tomorrow we're all going to make Christmas cookies and take them to Hope Retirement Home along with Mom's homemade eggnog. Now that, I have mastered."

"Even when my parents were alive we didn't have any traditions other than going to church on Christmas Eve."

"You're welcome to take part in our traditions. Miss Alice is going to help tomorrow with the cookies and go with us to deliver them."

"I wish I could, but I promised Pete I would help with some of his repairs at his house. He still has quite a bit of work to do on his place."

"Somehow I can see you doing that more than baking cookies," Kathleen said with a chuckle. "It's a lot of fun, but the real work starts after the cookies are boxed up and ready to go."

His forehead furrowed as he slowly moved forward in the line. "Taking them to the retirement home?"

"No, cleaning up the mess my boys make. Sort of like a mini hurricane blowing through the kitchen. You know flour goes everywhere and in places you don't want when you start throwing it at your brother."

"Interesting. I would never have figured that." His laughter filled the air.

Kathleen loved hearing him laugh. It invited her to join in on the merriment. She was falling for him, and she didn't know if that was a smart move. Her marriage problems were still so fresh in her mind. What if she made a mistake as she did with marrying Derek? She had more than herself to consider in this. As she reached her mom behind the first table of goodies, she shook the dilemma from her mind. She wasn't going to let worrying over it ruin her evening.

"Thanks for carrying Kip up to bed again. All this activity is wearing him out. It's hard to restrict him at this time of year." Kathleen opened the front door for Gideon.

He headed up the stairs with Jared following.

"Why does he always get to be carried up the stairs? I should have fallen asleep in the car on the way home, then you would have to carry me, too. Except I would like you to do a fireman's carry with me."

Gideon bit the inside of his cheek to keep from chuckling at the continual one-upmanship between the two brothers. At least he finally heard from *his* brother overseas. He would be returning to the United States in the spring and wanted to meet Gideon after all these years.

He had vague memories of times spent with Zach as children. Lighthearted, fun times. When he was living at some of the foster homes he'd been at, the atmosphere had been anything but lighthearted. Not all but a few—enough that he always watched his back and guarded his words.

Gideon placed Kip on the bed and covered him as he had the night they had decorated the Christmas tree. The simple action connected him to the child. He backed away, his emotions swelling in his chest, closing his throat.

"I'm going downstairs and probably fall asleep on the couch," Jared said at the doorway. "Remember the fireman's carry if I happen to fall asleep."

Gideon strode behind the boy. "Okay, but didn't your mom say something about getting ready for bed?"

He whirled around and began walking backward toward the stairs. "I didn't hear that. I'm not tired a bit."

"Well, then I guess you won't fall asleep on the couch."

He swung around and faced forward, grasping the banister. "I can get sleepy real fast."

"Okay, I'll keep that in mind."

Downstairs, Jared ran toward the den where the sound of voices was coming from. Gideon paused in the living room and stared at the tree. True to their word, the boys had filled almost all the blank places on the tree. He could hardly see the pine beneath all the decorations.

"Hi, I thought maybe you had gone home." Kathleen came up behind him and put her hand on his arm.

The touch zapped him with more feelings of wanting to belong to a family. "I wouldn't leave without telling you good-night. Besides, I have a sneaky suspicion that Jared is going to fall asleep on the couch in the den, and I'm going to have to carry him upstairs using the fireman's carry."

"You are? So now all I have to do to get him to sleep in the future is to have you here, ready, willing and able to carry him up the stairs over your shoulder. You're hired for the job."

He tweaked her pert nose. "It's a freebie." Hooking his arm around her, he pulled her close. "I enjoyed tonight. I've gone every year to the Lights On Celebration, but this year was special."

"Because we're celebrating more than the beginning of the holiday season. We're celebrating our comeback."

"I can see that you were a cheerleader in your youth."

She laughed. "I'm gonna take that as a compliment. Someone has to cheer people on. I'm very good at standing on the sidelines and doing that."

"Not participating?"

"In this case I guess I did. I still have paint under my fingernails and probably a splinter or two still in my hands."

He grabbed one of them and turned her palm up. "Where? I'm very good at taking out splinters. Show me and I'll get a needle and alcohol."

She snatched her hand back. "I think I'll take care of it. I still have one in my hand from when I was a little girl. It would take surgery to remove it now."

"I'm a trained paramedic. I probably could do that, too."

She snuggled closer. "Don't forget our date on the fifteenth. This is your chance to tell me what you want me to cook for you."

Enjoying her close to him, he looked over her shoulder and up. "Hmm. Let me see. Lobster and T-bone sounds great. Or..." He tilted his head, pretending to be in deep thought. "Actually, surprise me."

"No lobster and steak?"

"Nope. Although I do like seafood, lobster isn't my favorite."

"I think I have the perfect recipe in mind."

"What?"

"You wanted me to surprise you so I'm not telling you."

"That day I'll be at the doctor late. Do you want to use my kitchen earlier?"

"Probably would be better than me carting all the dishes to your house."

"Are you working that day?"

"No, and I will need all afternoon to prepare my feast." She grinned. "But that is all I'm telling you about what I'm preparing."

Their easy repartee only reinforced how comfortable he was with Kathleen. Her smile encompassed her whole face, joy radiating from her. He couldn't take his gaze off her mouth. Inviting. Tempting. He had to taste it.

He slowly lowered his head. "Thank you for this evening."

Her lips parted slightly, and he swooped in to kiss them. He pulled her against him, their rapid heartbeats matching tempos, and put everything into the merging of their mouths.

From afar, someone clearing her throat intruded into his dazed mind. He didn't want to end the kiss, but Kathleen disengaged and stepped from his embrace. She shifted to the right.

"Jared is asleep on the couch. He told me when he fell asleep I was to get Gideon. That he'd know what to do." Amusement laced Ruth's voice.

Bereft without her in his arms, Gideon nodded his head and clicked his shoes. "Duty calls."

The urge to tickle Jared was strong, but Gideon resisted it. He bent down and hoisted the child over his right shoulder. He weighed next to nothing considering some of the equipment he had to haul in a fire. Mounting the stairs, he sensed Kathleen's gaze on him. That awareness of her heightened an electric sensation that charged his nerves.

Then she was behind him, following him up

the steps. What would it feel like to carry his own child to bed, to have his wife accompany him and them both put him down to sleep? The way his life was going, he'd never find out unless he was willing to make a change and risk getting hurt again.

Chapter Twelve

As Kathleen sliced up the red pepper for a salad,
her hand shook. Finally, she lay it beside the cutting board and gripped the edge of the counter
in Gideon's kitchen. How was she going to find
the money for the medical bills for Kip? She was
still paying off her husband's debt. The doctor's
bill had arrived this afternoon, and it was worse
than she thought. She didn't even have the energy
to call the doctor's office to talk with someone
about what she owed. All her mistakes from her
past were crushing her, and she didn't know how
to get out from under them.

She forced herself to pick up the paring knife
and finish making the salad. The scent of shrimp
gumbo saturated the room with its spicy seafood aroma. The repetitive motion of dicing the
pepper up into small pieces didn't soothe as it
usually did. That was one of the reasons she en-

joyed cooking—she could forget her troubles for a while. But not this time.

Gideon would be home soon and ready to celebrate after having his cast removed today. And that was the last thing she felt like doing. She wasn't even sure how she was going to get enthusiastic about the holidays. She had purchased a couple of gifts for her boys before Kip's accident and the car repairs. That would have to be their Christmas. Although she was already working some extra shifts at the hospital, maybe she could find another nursing job. She didn't have anything else she could sell to raise money. Most of her possessions were gone in the hurricane. The more she thought about her mounting debt the more her movements slowed until she couldn't even lift the blade.

Tears blurred her vision, and she closed her eyes, setting the knife on the counter. She didn't have any answers to her problems. She'd thought about filing for bankruptcy, but she didn't want to do that if at all possible.

The sound of the front door opening then closing underscored she wasn't alone anymore. She needed to get her composure together. This was her problem, and she didn't want to burden anyone else, even Gideon, with it. She straightened, wiped the tears from her eyes and picked up the knife to complete the salad.

"Honey, I'm home," Gideon said as he came into the kitchen. "Now does that not sound like one of those shows in the fifties like *Leave It to Beaver* or *Father Knows Best?*"

She forced a smile to her lips and turned toward him. "I think, Mr. O'Brien, you've had way too much time on your hands."

"I beg your pardon. I've been working at a dull desk job."

"Which must have given you time to daydream."

"I did find myself drifting off every once in a while, but don't tell the captain." He held up his cast-free arm and waved it. "Now that I'm back on rotation, he'd have me doing twice the work."

"Poor guy. You can't have it both ways. Either desk duty or firefighter. Which is it going to be?" She began dicing the rest of the pepper.

"No contest—firefighter." He closed the distance between them and drew in a deep breath. "Ah, that's a great smell. Shrimp gumbo. How did you know that's one of my favorite dishes?"

"A little sleuthing on my part. I called Pete, and he told me."

"And he didn't say a word to me. I didn't think Pete could keep quiet about anything."

She smiled at him. "This time he did."

"Can I help you with anything?"

"You can put the French bread into the oven at 375 degrees. Everything else is done."

"Want me to set the table?"

"I already did. In the dining room."

Gideon gave a low whistle. "You are going all out."

"That's the only way to do something. I even brought two of Mom's china place settings."

"I'm feeling pampered, and all I had to do was go into a burning building and do my job."

She caught him watching her reaction to his words. "For your information I have forgiven myself weeks ago about my part in your injuries. You have convinced me I wasn't responsible."

"Good. I was ready to launch into my spiel again if I had to." He put the bread in the oven then moved toward the dining room. "I have one final touch to add to the table."

"What?"

He swung around at the doorway. "You are not allowed in here until it is time to eat."

"Okay. But that's not fair. This was my evening to do for you."

He headed out of the room. "Who said life is fair?"

Fair? No, it wasn't. Since before Derek's death, it had been one problem after another. When something went wrong, she didn't even have time to recover before another crisis occurred.

The tears threatened again. She swallowed them away, but her throat burned.

"All done. I had to lend my finishing touch to the table."

She picked up the bowl of salad. "I'm done, too. I'm going to put this on the table—"

He plucked it from her hands. "Your ploy won't work. I'll take the food in."

"While you're in there, bring the bowls for the gumbo. The bread should be done in ten minutes."

"Great. I'm starved." He stopped in front of her by the stove and grasped the wooden spoon to stir the pot's contents. Bending over the heat rising from the gumbo, he inhaled and held the breath for a long moment then released it slowly. "I love that smell. I've been wondering all day what you were going to cook and was regretting telling you to surprise me. I don't like surprises normally."

"Neither do I." She threw a glance toward the dining room.

"You only have a few more minutes to wait." He inched toward her. "I can think of a couple of things we could do to pass the time until the bread is done."

His eyes gleamed as they roved over her face. He reached up and brushed her hair behind her ears, his gaze glued to her mouth. Her heart plummeted. His smoldering look spoke to her feminine side, urging her to give in to the feelings he generated in her. She couldn't, shouldn't.

When he sought her mouth and touched his to hers, she knew she needed to break it off. Her heart refused to listen to common sense that said she should get her life under control before even thinking of becoming involved with a man. She surrendered, giving him a part of herself she didn't have to give.

When they broke apart, their breathing ragged, Kathleen quickly tried to recapture that elusive part of herself—her heart. She couldn't risk it right now. She could never ask another to take on the kind of debt she had. It was *her* problem. No one else's.

He framed her face between his hands, his eyes leaving a heated trail where they roamed. "This wasn't exactly how I pictured telling you this. I wanted something a little romantic. But here goes. Kathleen Hart, I love you. I have never said that to another woman. Ever. In these past two months you've become so important to me. I hope one day you'll agree to be my wife. You don't have to say anything right now because I know you need time, but please think about it. I want to be a father to Kip and Jared. I want to be a husband to you."

Each word seared into her. *No. Don't. I can't.* She stared at him, seeing the sparkle in his eyes slowly fade, the smile transform into a look of puzzlement. Still, she couldn't say anything. It wouldn't be fair to Gideon. Her problems weren't his. She couldn't...

She backed away. "You know how I feel about marriage. I had one bad marriage and that was enough. I never want that again."

"To be married or a bad marriage?" His terse voice sliced through the air.

"Both. Not now." She whirled around and started toward the doorway into the dining room. She needed to get out of here.

He stopped her with a hand on her arm and rotated her toward him. "Stay. We can talk about this."

"No, enjoy the gumbo." The scent of burning bread permeated the kitchen. She gestured toward the oven. "You'd better take the bread out."

When he dropped her arm and turned toward the stove, she fled, hurrying past the dining room table. A gorgeous bouquet of flowers—lilies, carnations and others she didn't recognize—infused the air with their sweet fragrance. On a plate was a present in a small box. Its sight spurred her to a faster pace.

This wasn't the time to give her heart to another—not with all the complication in her life. *He'll thank me later.* But as she left his house, that thought didn't comfort her one bit.

* * *

Gideon yanked the burning bread from the oven. In his haste, one of his fingers touched the hot pan. He dropped it and jumped back. Staring at the bread on the floor, he stood rigid from the emotions bombarding him as if he were being hit over and over from all sides.

She doesn't want to have anything to do with me. She might as well tell me to get lost.

This was the reason he didn't put himself out there. Anger vied with his hurt. He wanted to be mad at Kathleen. He needed to be. Otherwise, the hurt would win, and he would be back to how it had been after his parents' deaths. He wouldn't go there again. He'd fought to get where he was today.

Lord, what do I do?

After a long day putting in overtime, all Kathleen wanted to do was put up her feet and do nothing. But tonight was the time she'd set aside to finish baking some goodies for her gifts to family and friends. It was all she could afford to do. When she entered the kitchen with her two bags of groceries, she found her mother at the table with her two sons painting the Christmas plates the goodies would be placed on. She'd wanted to help with that part, too, but when the overtime opportunity came up, her mom said she'd love to assist Jared and Kip. It would be a treat for her.

"It's about time you got home, Mom," Kip said, holding up his work of art. "What do you think? This is for Sally."

In the center of the white plate, he'd painted a green Christmas tree and then put ornaments on it and lots of presents under it, much like the front of Miss Alice's huge card. "Beautiful. She's going to love it." Her cousin was still living with her mother at least for a few more months until her apartment building was rebuilt.

"I'm doing one for Gideon. What do you think about mine?"

All she saw was Jared's big grin as he showed her his plate with green rolling hills and a night sky with a brilliant star shining in it. "You've done a great job."

"That's the star the Wise Men followed. I remember Gideon telling me about it when we put the star on our tree." He tilted his head and furrowed his forehead. "Why haven't we seen him lately? He hasn't been down here in a week. I had to visit him to see him without his cast."

"Yeah, Mom, is he mad at us or something?"

Kathleen locked gazes with her mother. "I know he isn't mad at you two, but now that he can work as a firefighter again, he has needed to focus on that."

"I asked him to go to church with us on Christmas Eve." Jared set his plate down among the others they had painted. "He said he couldn't. It's sad he doesn't have a family to share Christmas with."

"Yes, it is," she murmured and turned away from her children before she started crying in front of them. She'd made such a mess of everything.

"We could be his family this Christmas," Kip said.

"That looks like the last two plates you need to do." Her mother glanced at the clock on the wall. "You said something about watching that Christmas movie on TV tonight. It'll be on in five minutes. You need to wash up and get into your pajamas. It'll be late when the movie is over and time for bed."

After her boys left the room, her mom approached her. "Are you all right?"

"No. Everything is falling apart. I—" Kathleen couldn't find the words to tell her mother how much she'd missed Gideon the past week. She glimpsed him once leaving his house, and it had taken all her willpower not to run after him and beg his forgiveness.

"I haven't wanted to pry—okay, maybe I have—but talking about what happened between y'all last week might help you."

"I had just gotten the final bill from the doctor and hospital for Kip's accident that day I made dinner for him. When he told me he loved me and—"

"He loves you! Why didn't you tell me? That's great. That's—" Her enthusiasm waned. "Is that the problem? You don't love him?"

"I do love him. I didn't want to fall in love, but this whole week he's all I thought about. I miss him terribly and yet, Mom, how can I ask a man to take on my debt, especially now that thousands more have been added to it? I can't. It's not his problem. It's mine."

"Did you talk to him about it?"

"No."

"Why not? He at least deserves to know you care about him, and why you don't want to see him anymore. You aren't being fair to him."

"I believe he told me life isn't always fair."

"That's a cop-out and you know it." Her mother sighed. "He's good with the boys. They deserve someone like him in their lives. From what you told me, their own father didn't pay much attention to them in the last few years before he died."

"Yeah, and both Jared and Kip have drunk in Gideon's attention."

"Did you think they wouldn't ask why he wasn't coming around?"

"I didn't think. I just reacted to him telling me

he loved me. I got scared. I still am. What if I make a mistake like I did with Derek?"

"Gideon is a good man. He is nothing like Derek. Whether he is for you is another question and one only you can answer. Do you want Derek to control the rest of your life? He will if you let what happened between you two dictate how you live now." Her mother took her hands. "Honey, you shouldn't be having this conversation with me but with Gideon."

"Have I told you lately how much I love you?" Kathleen hugged her. "I don't know what I would have done if I hadn't come home. I was a mess after Derek died. I should have come back to Hope right away."

"I tried to get you to."

"I know. I thought I was giving Jared and Kip what they needed. Stability. When what they needed was here all along."

"Go rest. You look beat. I'm going to make some brownies and divinity for your goodie plates. Then if you want to add anything besides the lemon bars you did last night, that's fine. The kitchen will be all yours."

Kathleen dragged herself up the stairs to her room where she was sure she would go to sleep immediately after falling into bed. But fifteen minutes later, she punched the pillow and flipped over onto her back. As she stared at the ceiling, she turned to the Lord for guidance. She needed help untangling the mess her life was in. He was the only one who could help her.

"Gideon, a lady is here to see you," Captain Fox at Station Two said as he came into the living area on Christmas Eve.

Through the open doorway, Gideon spied Kathleen standing in the bay where the fire trucks were parked. Wearing a red and green plaid dress, she looked beautiful. His heartbeat responded by kicking up a notch, and his stomach muscles cinched.

I don't want to see her. Who are you kidding? It's taken all you have to stay away from her. Not to storm down to Ruth's and demand she love you.

Gideon shoved to his feet and covered the distance to the exit, aware of his fellow firefighters looking on as he left, intense curiosity in their expressions. A woman didn't usually come to the fire station unless she was a wife of one of the firefighters on duty.

"Thanks, captain," Gideon said as he passed him.

When he emerged into the large bay, a cool breeze blew through the large open doors. Beyond Kathleen, Christmas lights shone in the darkness. He stopped a few feet from her.

Her smile transformed the tired lines of her face into a look of radiance. "I didn't realize you were working tonight. I'd gone down to your house to talk to you and see if you would go to Christmas Eve service and discovered you were working."

"I'm filling in for a guy who has a young family. He should be home tonight and tomorrow. I don't have anyone."

"Jared and Kip will be disappointed, but I can certainly understand."

"I'll be off tomorrow night. I'll come and see them then. I have some gifts for them. Is that where you're going now—to church?"

"Yeah, I'm going to meet Mom and the boys there. I told them I needed to come see you first."

"Why?"

She took a deep breath. "I had my speech all planned. That was why I had gone down to your house. But when you weren't home, it threw me off."

"You don't go with the flow much, do you?"

"I'm still learning." She turned toward a table to the side and picked up a plate with goodies covered in plastic wrap. "Merry Christmas. The boys decorated the plate, and Mom and I made the sweets."

"Thanks." He didn't know what else to say to her. He'd gotten her a heart-shaped necklace the day he'd gone to have his cast taken off. It still sat on his dresser, a constant reminder of the risk of falling in love. But he hadn't been able to bring himself to return it to the jewelry store. The couple of times he had tried he hadn't been able to do it.

Silence descended. Gideon took a step back. Kathleen looked out toward the street.

Seeing her only made him want to talk some sense into her. Or to drag her to him and kiss her senseless until she gave in to the feelings he knew she was beginning to have toward him.

"Well…" He searched for the right thing to say. "Tell the boys and your mom Merry Christmas for me. I'll be sure to drop by tomorrow evening." He backed away some more.

"Don't leave yet." Her chest rose and fell several times. "I—I was wrong with what I said the last time we saw each other. From the beginning I've been afraid of my feelings for you. After Derek's death I'd decided I didn't want to get married again. That I would focus on Jared and Kip. Then I met you and you changed everything. I love you, Gideon. I have no doubts about that."

He clenched his hands at his sides. "Then why did you say what you did?"

"Because earlier that day I had found out the extent of money I would owe for Kip's accident. Thousands of dollars added on top of the debt my husband left me. It was too much to process. I still don't know exactly what I'm going to do, and I certainly didn't want you to be drawn into it."

"Haven't you learned by now that it's okay to ask for help? The Lord didn't intend for us to go through life alone. It's taken me years to realize that. In fact, until I met you I didn't fully realize how alone I was. After my parents died, I lost hope of finding that connection I needed to fulfill my life. You and your family gave me that hope."

"And then that night I shattered it. I'm so sorry. I was afraid. Still am, but I had a long talk with God. I think He brought me here to Hope and to you because He wanted me to heal. I've been emotionally alone for many years, even before my husband died. I need you."

He closed the space between them. "I can help you. Together as a team we'll work it out. As a firefighter I've learned to be a team member. It hasn't always been easy because I kept those walls up. But this town, these people have helped me to break those walls down." He clasped her hands and drew her toward him. "You have. Let me be a part of your life. Fully. I'm in this relationship one hundred percent."

She wound her arms around his neck and dragged him down for a kiss. "How can I turn down an offer like that?"

He smiled and hugged her close to him. "I'm hoping you won't." He wouldn't be alone anymore. He had a family to care for and love.

Epilogue

The next evening Gideon arrived at Kathleen's mother's house with his arms full of presents. Jared and Kip were speechless as Gideon handed them their gifts. "Open them," he said as he sat next to Kathleen on the couch and took her hand.

Both boys tore into the packages, unveiling clothes and other items they had lost in the hurricane.

Glimpsing the joy on Gideon's face, Kathleen leaned toward him. "You shouldn't have. But thank you."

"They needed the clothes. I had so much fun shopping for them. And I threw in a couple of treats for them, too."

Jared held up his rock tumbler. "Yay! I have some rocks I've found that I can put in here. Can I tonight?"

Kathleen chuckled. "Somehow I figured you

would say that. We'll set it up in the garage so the noise doesn't drive us crazy."

When Jared and Kip had finished, sitting among the boxes and wrapping paper, beaming, Gideon rose and drew Kathleen up next to him. "I have one more surprise for you two."

Kip looked around. "Where?"

"On the porch." Gideon started for the front door.

Jared and Kip peered at each other then went after Gideon. Kathleen took up the rear.

Out on the porch sat two boys bikes—one red and the other blue. Her sons' eyes bugged out, both Kip and Jared rooted to the cement.

"The red one is Kip's and the blue, Jared's," Gideon finally said when they still hadn't moved.

Suddenly, they surged forward, clasping the handlebars of their bikes. "Thank you. Thank you," Kip said, then Jared.

Kip swept around and hugged Gideon. "Mom, can we go for a ride?"

"Yes, but only on the sidewalk. You can ride down to the end of the block and back."

Gideon helped Jared and Kip carry their bikes to the sidewalk, the Christmas lights from the neighbors giving off enough illumination for them to see where they were going.

When they took off, Gideon moved back next to Kathleen to watch, slipping his arm around her. "I haven't forgotten you." He drew her toward the steps where the porch light glowed and handed her a wrapped box lying on the wicker chair. "This is for you."

She carefully removed the paper then the lid, and lifted a gold chain with a heart dangling from it. "This is beautiful. I love it."

"You have my heart. I wanted you to have one to wear close to yours."

"Will you put this on for me?" She turned her back to him and lifted her hair so he could.

His fingers on her neck sent a thrill through her. After fastening the necklace, he bent forward and whispered, "That isn't the only surprise for you."

She glanced over her shoulder. "You're spoiling me."

"I want to spend the rest of my life doing that very thing." He turned her around and kissed her. "The mayor heard about your medical bills and wants to help. A fund has been set up to help you pay for Kip's accident."

Words refused to materialize in her mind. She stared at Gideon for a long moment, trying to comprehend what he told her.

Gideon shifted her toward him. "Are you all right?"

Thank You, Lord, for sending Gideon to me. "I'm more than all right. After all, I'm in love with a wonderful man."

* * * * *

Dear Reader,

His Holiday Family is the first book in the A Town Called Hope series. Hope, Mississippi, is a small town on the Gulf Coast that faced a hurricane. The series is about how a town rebuilds after a hurricane and grows stronger from its trials. I lived for many years on the Mississippi Gulf Coast and faced several hurricanes that hit my town. This is a tribute to all the people who assist people back on their feet after a tragedy.

I love hearing from readers. You can contact me at margaretdaley@gmail.com or at P.O. Box 2074 Tulsa, OK 74101. You can also learn more about my books at http://www.margaretdaley.com. I have a quarterly newsletter that you can sign up for on my website or you can enter my monthly drawings by signing my guest book on the website.

Best wishes,

Margaret Daley

Questions For Discussion

1. When tragedy strikes, who do you turn to? What do you do to solve the problems that arise from the tragedy—ignore it, figure out what steps you need to do or wallow in self-pity?

2. Kathleen began to doubt that the Lord cared about her. She'd prayed for help and didn't think she was getting any from Him. Have you ever thought that? What did you do?

3. Gideon lost so many people important in his life that he became a loner. He felt if he didn't care about others, he couldn't be hurt. Have you ever dealt with someone who emotionally kept his distance? What, if anything, did you do to break down his walls?

4. Who is your favorite character? Why?

5. What would you do if a hurricane (or any other tragedy) struck your home and took all your possessions?

6. Gideon learned as a firefighter to be a team player. Do you prefer doing things solo or with a team? Why?

7. Both Kip and Jared were not happy being moved to Hope. They were angry with Kathleen because they missed their friends and home in Denver. Did you have to move as a child? How did you adjust? What helps a child adjust to a move to another town?

8. Kathleen didn't feel she could accept help from Gideon. After her bad marriage, she thought that would be saying she was weak. Is it easy for you to accept help from people? If not, why do you have trouble with that? What are some ways people can get over thinking they have to do everything themselves?

9. What is your favorite scene? Why?

10. Kathleen had to learn to believe in herself again. She was afraid to trust her feelings developing concerning Gideon. Instead of letting herself care, she pulled away. She denied her feelings, thinking she was better off by doing that. Have you done that? Did it work? Why or why not?

11. Kathleen felt guilty for causing Gideon's injury. She had been conditioned and didn't know how to work her way through her guilt. It was one of the reasons she had reached a crossroad in her life. How have you dealt with guilt?

12. Kathleen and her family had certain traditions they did at Christmas. Are traditions in your life important to you? What are some that you and your family do?

13. Kathleen had a large debt to pay because of her husband's spending. She felt overwhelmed and wasn't sure how to reduce the debt. Have you faced money problems? What are some steps that could help Kathleen get out of debt?

14. When Gideon's house burned down as a young boy, he grabbed his baseball card collection that he and his father had collected. He treasured it because it reminded him of his father who died in the fire. What would you grab if your house was burning and why?

15. Kathleen rejected Gideon's love and hurt him. Gideon had never told another woman he loved her. It took a lot for him to do that. Sometimes we can't avoid being around people who have hurt us. What are some things we can do to deal with people who have hurt us?

LARGER-PRINT BOOKS!

GET 2 FREE
LARGER-PRINT NOVELS
PLUS 2 FREE
MYSTERY GIFTS

Love Inspired®

Larger-print novels are now available...

Love Inspired
SUSPENSE
RIVETING INSPIRATIONAL ROMANCE

Watch for our series of edge-
of-your-seat suspense novels.
These contemporary tales
of intrigue and romance
feature Christian characters
facing challenges to their faith...
and their lives!

AVAILABLE IN REGULAR
& LARGER-PRINT FORMATS

For exciting stories that reflect traditional values,
visit:
www.ReaderService.com